THE WAR OF
WALNEYRIA

JAMIE WEBER

LUCIDBOOKS

The War of Walneyria

Copyright © 2020 by Jamie Weber

Published by Lucid Books in Houston, TX
www.LucidBooksPublishing.com

eISBN: 978-1-63296-380-2
ISBN: 978-1-63296-883-8

Special Sales: Most Lucid Books titles are available in special quantity discounts. Custom imprinting or excerpting can also be done to fit special needs. Contact Lucid Books at Info@LucidBooksPublishing.com.

The Weber family would like to dedicate this book to Jamie's good friends who encouraged him in his writing: Brigit, Soda, Mason, Mac, Cherry, and many others.
We love you and thank you.
We hope this novel is read and enjoyed, but mostly we are proud of our Jamie Boy for getting it out into the world.

TABLE OF CONTENTS

CHAPTER ONE

The Tuesday Revolt started Walneyria on its path to war. A century ago, on September 9, 1952, 17 rebels launched an attack on the old royal manor, the seat of the corrupt monarchy. In a matter of minutes, they killed nearly every member of the royal guard and gravely wounded the tyrant king. The rebel leader stormed the manor with his soldiers, killed any remaining guards, and captured the king. After transporting the king back to the hidden camp, they tended his wounds so he wouldn't die too quickly and locked him in a small jail cell. The rebels made radio and television broadcasts across the nation, giving their demands to the citizens who could do nothing to save the king.

Five days later, on September 14, 1952, the rebels broadcast the king's execution across the country. Some cheered; most were horrified at the gruesome scene. The rebels burned the royal manor and took control of the legislative building. Nigel Frathwell, leader of the group, declared a democracy, making himself the transitionary president of Walneyria for the next 30 days. He kept his word, and 30 days later, he held an election. Every candidate was a member of the rebellion, but the people chose the person they considered the most level-headed and sensible. Nigel was the vice president, and the fledgling democracy soon gained more power and controlled the country relatively peacefully for the next century, with other citizens running for positions of power in later elections. What seemed terrible in the beginning worked out better for Walneyria since a true democracy formed. It became the only Walneyria my father grew up in and all we'd ever known.

Then, on October 27, 2051, Marcus Krisprelli, a confirmed heir to the old throne, returned to Walneyria and began a political campaign for the presidency. There was no one alive from the days of the Tuesday Revolt, no one who had witnessed the horrible power and corruption of the monarchy. No one understood what would happen if Krisprelli gained power.

A week later, Krisprelli was elected president of Walneyria. We later learned that he'd rigged the senate elections, allowing him to pass his first act as president: suspending democracy and reinstating the monarchy. The senators became his royal advisors, and Krisprelli immediately began ruling the country with an iron grip. He imprisoned anyone who said even one word that wasn't supportive of his regime. He executed those who whispered about how he'd rigged the elections. He spread propaganda, trying to cover up the mass imprisonments and executions.

Those of us who opposed his rule had to be incredibly careful and secretive to ensure we were not seen by spies. An underground opposition group formed, and we worked in secret to destabilize the rule of Krisprelli and to bring more people to our side. The Opposition's work was hard and incredibly dangerous, and our risk of death was extremely high if we were discovered. While the police largely did not support the king, they had to follow his orders or face imprisonment. In many ways, they were in just as much danger as the Opposition.

After about a month, the Opposition had grown to 53 members and changed their name to the Krisprelli Removal Party (KRP). They had not yet been discovered. They had destabilized the rule of the monarchy in two states of the kingdom, winning the favor of the governors who promised their support in return for a promise that violence from the Opposition would be prevented for as long as possible. It was an agreement easily made since the KRP did not intend to use violence until it was completely unavoidable. Our ultimate goal was to win the favor of the senators, now royal advisors, and have them oppose Krisprelli. But the nonviolent approach of the party could not continue as long as we had hoped. In the following weeks, more members joined the KRP, which won over more governors and further destabilized the king's rule across the nation.

I, Nate Mair, was elected president of the KRP. Samuel Dakota was the diplomatic advisor, Ava Moore was the chief engineer, and Freya West was our strategic planner. We were young—some might say too young—to be leading this rebellion. We would have been in the university had the war never started. But we had each stepped up when duty called, and age did not matter.

Initially, we were incredibly cautious about who knew our plans, only initiating conversations with others when they first showed dissatisfaction with the monarchy. We kept plans safe in our base and slowly grew our numbers. But as our membership grew, we were less cautious about who we trusted, and we were betrayed.

A member of the party revealed us to a senator, who then spread the word to the other senators and eventually the king. The king mobilized his army on the KRP's base, but the party was prepared. The governors who supported the party sent forth mercenaries and weapons they had stockpiled, along with the KRP's own fighters.

This battle marked the beginning of the Walneyrian Civil War. The clash between the king's army and the fighters of the KRP went on for several days before Krisprelli's advisors ordered a retreat. The KRP, now simply known as the rebels, had killed many of the king's men while suffering only two deaths and a few injuries of their own. The battle was a definitive victory for the rebellion but would come to have immediate, unimaginable consequences for the country. The states that the rebellion had won over declared independence from Walneyria, and the governors and rebel leaders held a meeting.

Lawrence Phillips, governor of Highborough, opened the meeting with roll call. "In attendance: Lawrence Phillips, Margaret Thompson, and Sylvestor Arnett, governors of the rebelling Walneyrian states. Nate Mair, Samuel Dakota, Ava Moore, and Freya West, leaders of the rebellion. Welcome to your new base, such as it is."

"Thank you, Mr. Phillips," Samuel said. "As we all know, the corrupt king of Walneyria launched an attack on our base in the state of Highborough. While we repelled the attack with minor casualties, this attack shows us that we must continue to fight against the corrupt king. If he will try to kill us before we have committed an act of violence against him, we have no idea how far he will go now that we have had to commit violence against him."

"The states of Highborough, Woodhollow, and Esterden will band together to form the Walneyrian Opposition, which shall be led by the governors of these states, along with the rebel leaders," Lawrence said solemnly. "This meeting shall mark the beginning of a civil war in Walneyria. All in favor say aye."

All those in attendance said aye in unison. We would not allow this violence against us to stand any longer. If Krisprelli would attack us before we incited violence against him, we had to act directly. We would work in the open to bring people and soldiers to our cause and to once again rid the country of Walneyria of an oppressive monarchy. While we did not want to resort to violence such as the Tuesday Revolt, if it were to come to such a point, we would commit every resource we had at our disposal.

We still didn't know who the double agent in the group was. All we knew was that because of his or her actions, the nation of Walneyria had been plunged into a civil war that would have innumerable consequences for the future of the nation and possibly the world as a whole.

The rebellion was being supported by Lawrence Phillips, Margaret Thompson, and Sylvestor Arnett, the governors of Highborough, Woodhollow, and Esterden, respectively. If it were not for the mercenaries and weaponry they sent us before the attack on our original base, we would have lost that battle. The governors declared the independence of the states they led, turning the conflict into a proper civil war. They allowed us to treat our wounded in their hospitals while we built a new base of operations in the capital of the newly formed Walneyrian Opposition States. As construction efforts went on, we got news that more and more Walneyrian citizens were fleeing to the Opposition States. More governors had declared the independence of the states they held power in—the states that had joined the KRP—and renamed it the Opposition.

It took nearly a month for our new base to be constructed. In that time, the Opposition grew to around half the states that made up Walneyria. Krisprelli's rule was steadily weakening, and he became more desperate because of it. He ordered the police to jail anyone who tried to evacuate to the rebelling states. He executed prisoners publicly, choosing who to execute at random simply to "set an example" for the populace. Some of his advisors, due to the growing madness and unpredictability of Krisprelli, elaborately faked their deaths to leave his court and flee to the Opposition. Krisprelli grew even angrier, slipped further into madness, and executed more of the numerous prisoners he had taken. He ordered the army to begin regular patrols around the country to prevent further migration into the Opposition States. We learned all of this from the advisors who had fled.

When we took in the advisors to protect them, Freya noticed that three of them had not fled with the others. We asked why they had remained, and they told us that two of the advisors still supported Krisprelli, and one was a spy for our side. We promised them safety in the Opposition and ensured them we would stop Krisprelli's twisted regime once we were able to. They promised us any help they could give to stop him. The war for Walneyria was in full swing.

CHAPTER TWO

We spoke with the senators for several hours, sharing information with one another. Samuel was skeptical about protecting them, but I ensured him it would be good for our side to keep them safe. I led the senators to their rooms and continued my activities around the base. Freya was creating battle plans and evaluating the uninjured soldiers, Samuel was evaluating the prospects who would reach out for help from neighboring countries, and Ava was repairing mechanical systems around the base. Samuel and I worked in the medical ward while the others went about their activities.

"Testing interbase communication system. Testing." Ava's voice broadcast across the speakers in the base. "Can anyone hear me?"

"We can hear you clearly. Could you report to the medical ward?" I replied through the small communication setup built into my room.

Although Ava was the engineer of the rebels, she had also practiced medicine in school. She combined her medical and technical skills to repair the medical equipment we were able to recover, allowing us to use it in the treatment of our injured people after the Battle of Highborough. Ava worked on the mechanical aspects of the new base whenever she was able to get away from the medical ward, but she had repaired nearly everything at this point. Samuel and I had been working in the med ward, along with some of the rebels who had not been injured in the battle, while Ava finished repairs on the comms system.

"I'm here. What do you need?" Ava spoke softly as she leaned inside the room.

"Some of the people in here need more blood," I replied. "We've been working as quickly as we can, but we need another set of hands."

Ava, Samuel, and I worked on giving more blood transfusions to the injured, allowing the others who had been helping us to rest. Those who had been gravely injured in the battle would need treatment for days, if not weeks. Thankfully, most of the injuries were light enough that treatment took only a few days. We all knew that this likely would not be the last time this room would be so full. It took several hours for us to treat everyone, and once we were done, Samuel stayed to watch the patients as Ava and I walked quietly out to Ava's workshop.

"I've been working on something you may find interesting. It would be quite useful for more . . . covert actions if the opportunity were ever to present itself." Ava spoke in hushed tones, as if she didn't want anyone to hear her speaking.

"What is it?" I cocked my head to the side and squinted at her.

Ava clutched my hand and pulled me toward a table tucked away in the corner of her workshop. Various tools and scrap pieces were scattered across the top. In the center of the table sat a gauntlet with a mechanism affixed to it I did not recognize. After inspecting the mechanism carefully, I picked up the gauntlet and strapped it tightly to my forearm. I took a closer look at the mechanism that was attached to it, being careful not to engage it because I had no knowledge of what it would do once activated.

Ava began to speak with clear joy about her work: "I took great care constructing this piece. The gauntlet itself was rather trivial, as I only needed to reinforce a leather gauntlet I already had. The true work of this piece is the mechanism that I notice you seem to have already been investigating. Make your hand into a fist; it should cause the mechanism to activate."

I did as Ava told me and made a fist with my hand. A blade extended out from the mechanism and over the top of my hand. It sprang out more quickly than I was able to see it, but it was constructed with enough care that my hand was uninjured. When I opened my hand, the blade retracted into the mechanism just as quickly as it had extended.

"I can see the opportunities this would create for us. How long did you spend on this?" I asked.

"The planning and drafting for the blade's extension and retraction mechanism took me several weeks. I had to be sure it worked properly and wouldn't injure its wearer. The actual construction took another week, just to be sure the mechanism would work properly. I began the project after the battle, with the intent we could use it during stealth missions or if we get close to a high-profile enemy and need an easily concealable weapon that doesn't create much noise. While the weapon wouldn't be incredibly practical in a traditional battle, it's still good to have available for certain opportunities, wouldn't you agree?"

"I can see several uses for this, yes. Perhaps we will have the chance to use it on Krisprelli himself in this war we've begun."

"That would be a most wonderful day for this nation," Ava responded. "I only hope we may all live to see the end of this conflict."

"As do I. For now, however, we must simply continue living the life we have been given and accept fate as it comes to us."

"Do you believe in everything we're fighting for, Nate? Have you considered we may ultimately be fighting for something that will fall into a doomed cycle? Will this country ever truly know a great, lasting peace in our lifetime? In our children's lifetimes? Or will our fighting pave the way for further fighting even long after we're buried in the bloodstained soil of our homelands?"

"Do any of us know if we're fighting the final great battle in this nation?" I said. "We're fighting for us, for the present. We all hope that we will be the end of this nation's bloodshed, but in the back of our minds, we all know that those who come after us will fight just as we have, but for different reasons than we hold for the battles we fight today."

"When we're older, when this war is behind us, when we're hopefully living in a freer, greater nation, when we're safe with families, I hope we look back on this, not with reverence but with great disdain." Ava looked remorseful. "Our actions should be considered disgusting, horrid things, done only because of a great desperation to free our fellow countrymen from the tyranny of a deranged, horrible king."

"I dislike what we've had to do just as much as you do," I said calmly. "The thought of what we'll have to do in the future concerns me just as much as what we've already done. But if we do not fight now, Krisprelli will continue his iron hold on Walneyria. When he takes back the states that formed the Opposition, he will hold them with an even more oppressive rule than he holds over the states that have not left Walneyria. We fight to defend their safety and to keep those lucky enough to flee to the Opposition States safe until we can take back Walneyria."

"I've just remembered some repairs I still need to make. Could you excuse me, Nate?"

"O-of course," I said, worried Ava had become upset with me because of what I had said. Ava had kept her head tilted downward as if to prevent me from seeing her face. She walked out of the room, but I stayed behind for a few minutes to allow her time to get some distance from the workshop. The following months would prove to be incredibly challenging times for everyone on the side of the rebellion, and doubly so for those of us at the top of the organization.

I walked to the planning room where Freya was creating battle plans. She had pasted maps on the walls, carefully marking rebel lands and Krisprelli-held lands along with troop placements, the patrols she and her scouts were able to observe, and carefully marked sniper positions. Freya had been a tactician for the military during a small-scale war between Walneyria and a neighboring country several years earlier, and the skills she had developed during that time led to the level of strategy she employed now.

As I walked inside, Freya turned toward the door and greeted me. "Nate, good to see you. I was hoping to discuss some of the plans I have come up with. The patrols of Krisprelli's army haven't deviated much since the Battle of Highborough, but our scouts are monitoring for alterations in their movements."

"And have we begun patrols of our own?"

"We have not. My fear is that if we were to do so, Krisprelli's soldiers would use the opportunity to easily harm our men, if not kill them outright. I am not one to shy away from a fight, but we do not need to give the enemy more opportunities to kill our fighters."

"I agree with you entirely, but if we do not begin patrols or even launch our own offensives against Krisprelli, we have no hope of making progress in this war."

"I understand what you're saying, Nate, but . . ." Freya was interrupted by Ava bursting into the room with a distressed look.

"They've taken Goldheart! They're making progress toward us right now. We need to fight them before they make it to us." Ava spoke quickly, obviously frightened.

"Damn it! Goldheart was one of our most strategic holdings. I'll get the soldiers ready."

I gathered Ava, Samuel, and some of the healthy rebel members and joined Freya with our soldiers, such as they were. Trying to calm everyone's nerves, I gave a quick speech to encourage them before we marched into battle. Samuel and Ava would remain at the base while Freya and I would fight with the others. This war became yet more trying on all of us.

CHAPTER THREE

By Freya's count, we had 427 able-bodied soldiers to fight Krisprelli's Royal Army. Based on our scouts and footage from surveillance drones, there were 600 Krisprelli soldiers in the attack on Goldheart, and there were hundreds more if he needed them. We were easily outmatched in any battle when it came to sheer manpower alone, even more so when it came to actual training and supplies.

But that didn't matter to any of us. None of us were afraid of that fact. We fought just as hard as anyone else would and could in this kind of situation. Our people had escaped a country consumed by fear and tyranny. Their fighting wasn't just for themselves and their own futures—it was for everyone in the country they called home.

Ava and Samuel would watch the fight from the base through the drones Ava had been able to repair. Freya and I got ready for the fight, along with the others who would be fighting. We all had armor, a pistol, and a rifle—and we were lucky to have them since much of our supplies had been lost during Highborough. Luckily, we had received more supplies as more states began to oppose Krisprelli's regime.

Freya was running an equipment check before we left the base, while Samuel and Ava had already gone to the surveillance room where the drone controls and live video feeds were set up. I quietly made my way to Ava's workshop, picked up the gauntlet with the blade mechanism, and put it on. I was unsure how useful it would be in a proper battle, but I wanted to have it in case something happened and I had no other weaponry available. I hurried back to where Freya and the soldiers were, and we left the base.

The march to Goldheart was not an incredibly long one since it was the neighboring state to Esterden where the rebel base had been built. Our snipers made it to the nearby high ground, while the rest of us marched onward into Goldheart. The entire state had been overrun with Royal Army forces, but their foothold in the region was the capital city of Swindance, an industrially focused town. Goldheart had not officially joined the Opposition States, but they had been sending their support to us in secret, trying to hide it from Krisprelli and his forces. It would seem, however, that their actions had been discovered, leading to the Royal Army's assault on the state.

"Are you ready?" Freya's voice came through the speaker in my helmet.

"Yes," I quickly replied.

Freya signaled the snipers, who quickly took out the snipers from the Royal Army and the more heavily armored troops on the ground. I ran to cover, as did everyone else, and engaged more of the Royal Army forces. Their numbers seemed innumerable as the fighting continued. The battle stretched on for hours before our numbers began to appear equal, though we were hit with several injuries.

But the fighting continued as we killed more of Krisprelli's soldiers. We began to suffer deaths of our own—injuries that could not be treated soon enough or shots that were an immediate death. My arm had been shot, but I was lucky that it was shot from a pistol that only damaged the armor I was wearing. The fighting went on for so long that I began to run low on ammunition, but Krisprelli's forces had fallen to low enough numbers that I had a plan.

"Freya, order our people to hold their fire." I spoke quietly through my helmet microphone.

"What? Why should I do that? We've almost won this fight!"

"Just trust me, please?"

Freya signaled our troops to stop shooting, and I made my way toward Krisprelli's forces. I was able to get behind one man and, swinging my arm as if to throw a punch, I stabbed him using the gauntlet blade Ava had built. His armor was relatively light but strong enough that it would stop a blade. However, the design of the armor left enough of a gap between the head and shoulders that a blade could go through it.

"Was that the gauntlet blade I built? When did you take it from the workshop?" Ava's voice cut through my helmet's speakers.

"I retrieved it shortly before we left for Goldheart in case a situation occurred in which I needed to use it. And, well . . . the situation occurred."

"Goddamn it, you reckless idiot! That wasn't intended for use during an active battle. You could have gotten killed."

"But I wasn't."

"That isn't the issue here."

I turned off the helmet's communication system and kept sneaking around, looking for the rest of Krisprelli's soldiers who had remained in Swindance. They continued to shoot at the rebels, but there weren't enough of Krisprelli's soldiers left for their gunfire to be overwhelming. I continued to carefully make my way around the battlefield, killing Royal Army soldiers as I found them until none remained. Turning the communications system back on, I alerted Freya, "That's all of them. We won this fight."

"They still have soldiers dispatched across Goldheart. Swindance is in Opposition hands, but the state is still under control by Krisprelli's regime. We'll need to keep fighting to take Goldheart fully into Opposition hands."

"How many soldiers do we still have who can fight?"

"By my estimates, around 394. All things considered, we did rather well in this battle."

"We'll bring the injured back to base and the dead to the cemetery for burial. One hundred of our men should remain here in Swindance to defend the area, and the rest of us will return to base to rest and decide further plans. We cannot allow Krisprelli to establish a proper foothold in Goldheart."

"I agree with you entirely," said Freya. "Krisprelli's presence in the rest of Walneyria is already frightening. If he were to retake a rebelling state . . . I dread to imagine what he would do to it."

We marched in silence during the rest of the trip back to Esterden, carrying the wounded and dead until a few trucks came to pick us up. I assumed either Samuel or Ava had sent them for us, as they had been watching us throughout the entire battle from the surveillance room. Freya took care to carry the dead to the cemetery, and I rode with the rest to the base where we carried the injured to the medical ward and performed any kind of urgent care necessary.

After we treated the injured, those who were helping me returned to their rooms to rest while I joined Ava and Samuel in the surveillance room. Ava was tinkering with the computers while Samuel was editing various documents he had prepared days ago. Ava jumped up from what she was working on and ran over to me, pulling my gauntlet off with a displeased expression.

"How could you do something so foolish? You could have gotten injured or even killed out there!"

"I did what I had to. If I didn't use it to neutralize those Royal Army soldiers, we would have gotten killed."

"Freya and the other soldiers still had ammunition for their weapons, Nate. What you did was a careless maneuver simply to show off to everyone else. What would we have done if you had been injured? Did you think about what would happen if you were killed or captured?"

I saw her point, but I was stubborn. "I'm prepared to give everything I can to support our efforts. Aren't you?"

"I'm just as prepared to give my life to our cause, but I will not let it happen by doing something so foolish such as you did today. Something terrible could have happened so easily, and you did it as if it were no big deal. You're still treating it like nothing! I will support you in everything you do, but I beg you to be more thoughtful from this point on."

"I will admit my actions today were careless, but sometimes a little carelessness is necessary in victory. If we were always overly careful, we would not strike at the enemy when we had the chance. We would stay defenseless, waiting for them to attack us. Would that not be worse than attacking, even if it were careless?"

"Carelessness is not something we can afford to dedicate ourselves to in times of war. We need careful battle plans, careful strategy and tactics, not rushing into battle without enough forethought to weigh the risks against the benefits."

Just then, Freya entered the room. "Ava is right, Nate. While what you did today worked out, it just as easily could have gone completely wrong. We can't allow you to do something like that again. As for everyone else, I believe a good bit of rest is in order after a day like today, wouldn't you agree?"

Ava, Freya, Samuel, and I walked quietly to each of our rooms. I lay there in bed, staring up at the ceiling, thinking about everything that had happened today. My actions were foolish—reckless. I should have realized that then. But they had happened. I was still here, those royal soldiers weren't, and Swindance was in Opposition control. We'd need to mobilize a full conquest of Goldheart to take it from Krisprelli's control. How long would it be until I once again saw a day of peace?

CHAPTER FOUR

I awoke the next morning to Freya contacting me through the comms station in my room. She spoke quickly, barely allowing me to keep up with her speech. I jumped up and rushed to the communication setup, tapping out a coded message to ask her to speak more slowly. Freya could translate code in her head, a skill she had developed during her time in the military, so I didn't need to wait for her to translate it before she began to speak at a more reasonable speed.

"We received more supplies from the Opposition States and are preparing everything before we mobilize the liberation of Goldheart. I'm putting you with the divisions that we're sending to take back Thompsonville, as Krisprelli's forces have established a foothold there. I will be going with the other divisions to take back Frostmorden, which is barely defended. Our troops in Swindance have reported back to us, telling us it has been easily defended."

"And what do we do once we take these cities into our control?" I asked. "Surely, we won't have control of Goldheart that easily."

"Through surveillance with Ava's drones, we were able to find out that Swindance, Frostmorden, and Thompsonville were the three largest towns in Goldheart with the presence of Royal Army forces. There are smaller patrols marching throughout the region, but if we can take and hold these three towns, we'll have the biggest part of the liberation down, and we'll only need to deal with the patrols across the state. Goldheart would be in Opposition control."

"How many times will we have to do that?" I asked. "Taking cities, liberating states, killing soldiers? How long will this war go on until we can rest easily once again? When will the bloodshed of this nation cease?"

"Soon, hopefully. Once we can put an end to Krisprelli and as soon as the Opposition holds the capital of Walneyria, we will be able to declare the end of this war and return to the regular, unremarkable lives we led before this started."

"And what if we don't live to that day? What if our lives are cut short before we can see the day when this country is not stained with the blood of its citizens?"

"Then we will have given our lives for something we all believed in," Freya said firmly. "If it takes our lives to keep thousands of other lives intact and free, then it will have been worth our deaths."

"So many of our people have already died for our cause. So many more of Krisprelli's men have died, too. The freedom of this nation is backed with the deaths of so many people, and even more of us will die before we once again see a single day of peace in our time."

"Freedom is never something easily won," she said, "and it's never something that's simply given to you. Throughout all history, freedom has been something we've fought for and fought hard to win. That's something that's not any different for us than it was for those before us. I want this war to be over just as much as any of us do, but the fighting must continue until Krisprelli is dead or refuses to send his soldiers to fight us."

"Both would be ideal, I think."

"Let's focus on what we need to do right now, Nate. Come to the barracks. Samuel and Ava are already in the surveillance room."

I made my way to the barracks as Freya asked me to do, joining the rest of our soldiers. Some of them had been injured in Highborough, so I was pleased to see they had healed enough to be able to fight once again. I wondered how many of them would live to see the end of this conflict they were fighting. All of them? A hundred? None of them? How many thought about their chances of dying? How many truly cared about that risk?

"Nate." Freya pointed toward the group of soldiers on the left side of the room as she continued speaking. "These are the divisions that will join you in taking back Thompsonville. The other divisions will come with me to Frostmorden. Everyone is already in their gear. Once you're ready, we'll head out."

Pulling on my armor, I noticed Ava had repaired the spot where my arm had been shot. I brought a medical kit with me, along with my rifle, pistol, and enough ammo to last for hours of fighting. In my helmet, I connected the communications network to Freya's so we could communicate with each other when we were separated.

"Ready to go, then? I'll keep contact with you during our march to Frostmorden. I expect you to do the same as you fight in Thompsonville. There are large numbers of Royal Army forces in Thompsonville, likely more than we faced in Swindance, so be prepared. Your snipers should get to any high ground available and watch for enemy snipers, as well as take out any of the more heavily armed and armored RA forces. Understood?"

Before I could reply on my own, the other soldiers in the room quickly answered to voice their understanding of what Freya had said. We left the barracks quickly, several soldiers walking with me on the path to Thompsonville, the others going with Freya to Frostmorden. We had walked about halfway to Thompsonville when Freya's voice came through the comms system: "We've nearly made it to Frostmorden. My snipers have already gotten to high ground and have reported little RA activity as far as they can see. What is your status?"

"We're getting close to Thompsonville," I said. "Snipers are looking for high ground as we get closer. I'm currently unsure of the level of RA activity. I'll inform you once we've gotten closer."

"Understood. Do not engage the enemy until everyone is in cover. Allow the snipers to make the first shots."

We continued making our way to Thompsonville, and our snipers made their way to high ground. Ava had built grappling hooks into their armor, allowing them to easily get to higher ground. Everyone else got into cover, or as close to cover as they could get. I gave the signal to our snipers, and their shots rang out as heavily armored RA soldiers and their snipers dropped to the ground before us. I radioed to Freya that the fighting had begun, but I got no response. I thought little of it and continued to fight, taking down Krisprelli's soldiers one by one, side by side with my fellow Opposition members.

The fighting lasted approximately three and a half hours until the RA forces retreated from Thompsonville, allowing us to declare the fight a victory. I looked around at the soldiers and saw a few with injuries, but luckily, we had suffered no deaths. I went around and treated the injuries with supplies from the medical kit I had brought, while other Opposition members did the same. Ava would perform more proper treatment once we returned to base. I once again tried to speak to Freya but still received no response.

Freya always responded to communications unless she was physically unable to. I began to assume the worst, and just then, a group of Opposition soldiers came rushing to us, carrying someone. The person they were carrying did not seem to be dead—at least not yet—but was seriously wounded. As the soldiers got closer, I saw who they were carrying.

It was Freya. One of the soldiers who was with the Frostmorden group told me that Freya was shot by a sniper who our own snipers were not able to see. The shot had completely pierced her armor. One of our snipers killed the sniper who shot Freya soon after he deduced where the shot had come from by the sound from the shot. Another soldier told me they had taken out most of Krisprelli's soldiers stationed in Frostmorden, but because some enemy soldiers remained when Freya was shot, a large numbere of Opposition soldiers stayed in Frostmorden to clear out the RA forces.

One hundred of the soldiers who had come with me to Thompsonville stayed behind to protect it from Krisprelli's forces. The rest of us carried Freya back to Esterden as quickly and carefully as we could. Ava quickly joined us and began emergency treatment on Freya to save her. The Opposition members who had a more in-depth knowledge of medical practice were able to aid Ava in her work more than I would have been able to.

Ava worked for hours to treat Freya, a task clearly not easy for her to do. I stayed in the medical ward to monitor Freya's status as Ava performed surgery on her. After several hours, Ava stepped away from the operating table and carefully lifted Freya, carrying her to a bed to set up a blood transfusion and IV.

"She'll make it, but her recovery will take quite some time," Ava said. "She's incredibly lucky the bullet didn't hit any of her vital organs and that the lasting impact should be relatively minor. She won't be up and walking around for at least a week, likely even longer than that. She'll still be able to create battle plans and tactics, but actually going out on the battlefield will be out of the question for quite some time."

"How long until she's awake again?"

"I wouldn't expect her to be awake for another several hours. You should stay here and watch over her until she wakes up, just to make sure she doesn't try to stand up. I'll tell the others to check in from time to time in case you fall asleep. I should tell Samuel, too."

"Thank you, Ava, for everything you've done for us."

Ava smiled at me and walked out of the room, presumably back to the surveillance room to tell Samuel. I stayed behind to watch over Freya and make sure her vital signs didn't change unexpectedly. We'd already lost so many good people in this war. What would we do if we were to lose someone as important to the Opposition as Freya? Even though she was a strong person and would pull through this, this occurrence pulled me back—or at least closer—to reality.

Nothing is safe in war. Everything you know, everyone you care about, all of it can be taken from you in an instant. Our country as we knew it didn't exist anymore, and it never would again. From now and forever, Walneyria would be scarred by the effects of this war. Walneyria was a nation forever changed by the ripple effects of the actions of just a handful of people. We lived in a new Walneyria than the one we had grown up in. And that thought was truly frightening to me.

CHAPTER FIVE

I stayed by Freya's side for several hours as she continued to rest. Some of the people in the base who knew proper medical procedures checked in from time to time, monitoring Freya's vitals and changing the blood and IV bags. There was little I could do besides watch Freya and wait for her to wake up. Ava told me she had lost consciousness due to shock, which only added to how lucky it was that she was carried back in time to be saved.

Mortality is not something you consider at many points in your life. It's not something many would want to think about from day to day. What is the point of worrying yourself by considering the inevitability of death? That was how I thought of it before the war began. When you are involved in a war such as this, especially when you are one of the people chiefly responsible for beginning it, the prospect of your mortality is something you begin to face more every day. It grows closer to reaching you as you stay only mere inches away from its terrible, cold embrace.

Freya always struck me as someone able to stay several feet ahead of that embrace. I'd never met anyone as strong and unwavering as she had always been. Yet with a single bullet, Freya had joined the rest of us in running from mortality, her lead cut down from feet to inches, and it grew ever shorter. For now, however, death would have a hell of a time chasing after her once she began to recover.

Ava came into the medical ward around 5:30 in the morning to check on Freya. She worked carefully, checking Freya's vitals and replacing the IV. When I checked the clock again, nearly 30 minutes had passed before Ava had finished. She went around to the other injured or otherwise unwell people in the medical bay, which took her another half hour. Once done, she walked back and sat in the chair beside me.

"Freya's recovering well. There's nothing abnormal in her vital signs, and we were able to replace the blood she lost. She shouldn't need any more IVs after this one, either, and should regain consciousness again soon." Ava spoke calmly.

"How long until she should be up and walking again?"

"I'd say she'll need a few days rest at least, maybe even a week. Even then, anything beyond walking around the base will be difficult for quite some time. We're quite lucky to still have her alive, especially since she'll suffer a relatively minor amount of lasting damage."

"You did an incredible job in your work to save her. I dread to think where we would be without your medical expertise."

"Realistically, you'd be digging more graves."

Samuel walked into the room and sat in a nearby chair. He handed me a small, yellowed envelope, seemingly sealed with wax. Closer inspection revealed it to be Krisprelli's crest, the symbol of a horrid man. I slowly opened the envelope and pulled a folded letter from it that said this:

> To the members of the Walneyrian Opposition, my name is Fredric Solsthar. I am the senator who remained in Walneyria to work as a spy. As you already know and have acted on, the rebel actions of Goldheart were discovered, causing Krisprelli to send forces in the region and take it into his control. You did well taking

Thompsonville, Swindance, and Frostmorden from his forces, but he won't give up that easily. He's sending more forces to Swindance within the next three days. Send more of your forces to the city to defend it, and perhaps you could send troops to Thompsonville and Frostmorden as well to make it less evident that you were sent information.

Carefully folding the letter again, I slid it into the envelope before handing it back to Samuel. I considered the words cautiously. With Freya injured, it would be necessary for me to act as the military commander for the Opposition during her recovery. My immediate thought, however, was to confirm the legitimacy of the letter with the senators under our protection. It was likely they could recognize Fredric's handwriting and tell us if the letter matched or did not match his handwriting.

"Have you talked with the senators about this letter, Samuel?" I asked.

"No, why would I do that?" Samuel asked with a strange defensiveness.

"I assume Nate wants to confirm it was actually written by the person who claims to be the writer," Ava replied before I could.

"Yes, that's right," I added. "I assume they would know if the handwriting matches Fredric's."

"There is no reason for us not to check," Samuel replied as he stood up. "Let's go find out."

We walked to the rooms the senators had taken as their own and gathered the five of them together. They read the letter carefully, and none of them showed obvious signs that it wasn't from Fredric. Once they finished, I slid the letter back into my pocket and questioned the senators.

"Does the handwriting of this letter match Fredric's?"

"It does," a few of the senators spoke up together.

"Then it's safe to assume that this letter is an accurate warning for the Opposition, correct?"

"There would be no reason to assume it is false."

"It's good to have confirmation. Thank you, Senators."

Samuel and I left the room, allowing the men to return to their rest. We then went to the barracks, gathering several soldiers and assembling them into groups. After making sure everyone was properly equipped and giving them their stations, we sent 100 of them to defend Swindance, while two groups of 50 went to Thompsonville and Frostmorden, disguising the fact that we had gotten word from Fredric.

I did not accompany our soldiers as I normally would because I would be needed at the base while Freya recovered. Ava had returned to her workshop to resume work on one of her projects, while Samuel and I sat in the medical ward to monitor Freya.

"What result do you want out of this war, Nate?" Samuel's voice broke the silence.

"I want to see the end of Krisprelli and his regime. I want to see Walneyria return to the peaceful democracy it had been since before we were born. I want to create a nation where we can be happy and safe, one where we don't have to worry about our day-to-day safety. That's what I want."

"You don't wish for power like Nigel Frathwell and his group from the original revolt?"

"Frathwell isn't a man I envy in any sense. His rebellion killed for the sake of killing. His elections included only his band of rebels. When this war is over, I will declare an immediate election that I shan't even be a candidate for. The people will decide which person they wish to rule over them during peacetime."

"I will admit that is an admirable stance, Nate, but is it one I'll be able to hold you to? Or will you go against your word and declare yourself the leader of Walneyria once you've put your blade in Krisprelli's back?"

"I will be back in my home living my life as I did before the war as soon as Krisprelli falls dead before me. You can count on that."

Samuel seemed to have little to say after my final remark, and I let the silence grow between us. Samuel was a man I admired, even if his personality seemed hostile at times. He was an inquisitive, secretive, untrusting man, and it took quite some time before he could trust anyone—for even now he doubted me at times. But what he lacked in trust he made up for in the skills of negotiation and diplomacy—hence his role as diplomatic advisor.

Ava walked back into the ward after some hours had passed. Samuel had fallen asleep in his chair while I continued to watch Freya. I watched as Ava carefully injected Freya with a small needle. She then sat in the chair next to me and waited.

I asked quietly, "What did you inject her with?"

"A nervous system stimulant I created. The effect is weaker than adrenaline, but it should aid Freya in regaining consciousness."

We continued to wait several more minutes until Freya began to slowly blink and open her eyes. Ava nearly jumped out of her chair and hurried to the bed, making sure Freya did not move too quickly. I hurried to the bed as well, glad to finally see Freya awake once again. She began to speak slowly, as if she had only just noticed that she was in the medical ward.

"What happened to me?"

"You got shot in Frostmorden. You were rushed back here, and Ava worked as quickly and carefully as she could to save you."

"How long have I been out?"

Ava looked at the clock and replied, "Around a day and a half. You'll need to spend more time in here to recover. Even just walking around the base will be difficult for you once you've regained enough strength. Going out for any fights will be completely impossible for quite some time."

"What's happened in Goldheart since I was injured?"

"Our spy sent us a letter telling us that more of the RA will be attacking Swindance in the next few days. We sent more soldiers there to defend the town. Additionally, we sent soldiers to Thompsonville and Frostmorden to hide that we received the information."

"We'll have to keep fighting hard to completely take Goldheart. Ava, would it be possible to wheel me to the surveillance room to watch the fighting once it begins?"

"If you have a couple more days to recover, it will be okay for you to go around the base in a wheelchair."

"Wonderful! It would be a shame to miss watching a good battle." Freya smiled weakly.

Ava gently nodded at Freya and walked back to her workshop. Samuel was still asleep, so I stayed by Freya's side to keep her company. Even after being injured, Freya didn't seem to waver in strength at all. She was still Freya, the same resilient, wonderful person I had always known. She wouldn't let this keep her down for long.

Freya and I talked a few more minutes until she needed to rest again. Then I went back to my room and sat at my desk. We didn't have computers in our rooms since most of the computers we had were in the surveillance room or medical bay, with a few in Ava's workshop to aid in her projects. I began writing absentmindedly in a notebook I had, but the words were mostly nonsense sentences I strung together. The past several days had been mentally exhausting to go through, but seeing Freya awake and acting like her normal self was a relief.

I wondered how much longer I could continue to fight, how much longer I could live and go through this war. Violence and bloodshed had become nearly daily events, and yet they didn't seem to get easier. I lay on my bed, thinking about the things I had seen, how horrible they were. Sleep came over me as the images played through my mind.

CHAPTER SIX

I rose from my bed slowly as sunlight streamed through the slats of the window covering in my room. I had been restless that night, with my dreams plagued by crimson-covered visions, some of them memories, the rest nightmares or perhaps premonitions of things yet to come. Unlike the past several days, I had not been awakened by a call but rather from sleep leaving my body. I decided to head to the medical ward to check on Freya.

In a way, it was funny how empty the halls felt since many of us were housed in the building. Maybe I had secluded myself from the world for so long that it began to seclude itself from me. The passage of time had always seemed to do nothing other than make everything lonelier for me. Time takes from you the people you love; it takes their health and their lives until it comes for you, too. Mortality and time, eternally intertwined, work together to take everything from you and never allow you even one day when life isn't slipping away. No one can escape that path, regardless of the tenacity of their efforts.

As I entered the ward, I noticed Samuel and Ava did not seem to be around, and Freya was sleeping. I sat on one of the chairs and read from a book on the table. It was uninteresting and served as little more than a way to pass time while waiting. But it would be my first choice in the event we needed fire kindling. The hands on the clock moved as slowly as ever, but they never moved slowly enough for me.

Freya woke up after a while and noticed me sitting beside her. She took time to sit up, clearly still a difficult task for her. After taking a sip from the cup beside her bed, she turned toward me, taking care to think of her words before she spoke.

"Has Krisprelli sent more of his troops to Swindance yet? What of our own troops? Are they well?"

"The RA hasn't marched on Swindance yet; it's still in our hands for now. Our soldiers are doing well. They've held Thompsonville and Frostmorden, too. Goldheart is still in our control, save any RA patrols we haven't taken out."

"That's good to hear. How have Ava and Samuel been?" Her voice was clear but weak.

"They've been doing well. Worried about your recovery, of course, but they're well."

"Ah, they needn't worry about me. I'll be back on my feet as soon as I can without collapsing to the floor."

"Hopefully, that won't be too long from now."

Freya had always been one to use humor to lighten the mood in situations like this, but even then, I was surprised by her joke and how calm she was in general. She had been involved in war before, which likely helped instill in her a general sense of calm. Had she become ambivalent to things like this, or was she just trying to help me stay calm?

"What are you thinking about, Nate?" I must have been silent for longer than I'd thought for Freya to notice.

"How are you able to stay so calm? Even in our situation, even after nearly getting killed, you seem so much calmer than I could ever be."

"I've had more time and opportunities to be faced with these scenarios than you have. I've nearly died several times, although this is the closest I've come to it." She looked down at her legs. "But the idea of death isn't something that scares me. Does it scare you?"

"In a way, it does. But I don't just view death as an event that comes to all of us. Growing up, I began to personify death and mortality.

To me, it's something constantly chasing after us while we have the slimmest lead against it. However, it doesn't chase only us; it chases everything we care about. It takes those close to us until it's able to take us, too."

"Is that what scares you? The being you've created in your mind to personify the certainty of death?"

"I would say that it is, yes. It isn't the inevitability that scares me but rather that it takes everyone close to us as we're evading it."

"In another life, you could have been a philosopher." Ava spoke quietly as she walked into the room, dragging a fairly large box behind her.

"What's in there?"

Ava responded to my question not with words but by opening the box and pulling out what appeared to be a metallic skeleton to wrap around a person's legs. She then took out a small, circular piece of tech and put it on the back of Freya's neck.

"What is that?" Freya asked after Ava had put it on her.

"It's linked to this." Ava pointed to the metal skeleton. "I built it in order to allow you to walk around the base. It will still be rather straining for you, but you'll at least be able to move around for short distances on foot."

Ava carefully picked up the skeleton and put it around Freya's legs. She then attached several panels of smooth metal to the skeleton, making it appear more like a robotic pair of legs, which in a way they were. Ava kept working, making small adjustments I could barely see, until she stepped back with a smile on her face. She helped Freya sit up in bed and then stand upright.

"Walking with these will be no different than walking around normally. I'd advise you to take it easy with your movements since you're still quite early into recovery. Let's walk back to my workshop for now."

Freya, Ava, and I walked out of the ward without saying much, walking slowly to not put too much strain on Freya. The medical ward was not a far walk from Ava's workshop, but it was far enough to make sure the apparatus worked properly. Once we made it to the room, Ava helped Freya onto one of the chairs.

"How do they feel?" Ava asked. "I have been working on the design for quite some time but did the finishing touches after you were hurt. The neural interface is easily one of my most advanced constructions yet." Ava barely tried to hide the pride in her voice.

Freya stretched out the new limbs. "They feel like legs. There isn't much I can say about them beyond that. I'm grateful you constructed them for me. Maybe once this war is over, you could research this technology further and make it on a wide scale to help others."

"That was why I began my research into the tech initially. I wanted to make it to help my dad before . . . " Ava's speech trailed off.

I remained quiet as Freya stood up and hugged Ava. Before the Opposition began its earliest work, Ava's father had been killed by Krisprelli's regime. His death was Ava's main motivation for joining the Opposition. Several of us had lost our friends and family to Krisprelli and his regime. We fought in honor of our fallen.

Ava began to tear up as she spoke. "I keep wondering if he'd be proud of me now. Would he be proud I was trying to help so many people, or would he be disappointed at the blood we've shed for our cause?

"He'd be incredibly proud of you and what you've done for us," Freya reassured Ava.

"Would everyone we've lost be proud of what we've done? We've taken the lives of so many people and lost the lives of several Opposition members in the process. Would my family be proud of me now, or would they despise me?"

Almost everyone we loved was buried now, and we'd have our questions until the day we died.

"Oh, there you are," Samuel said as he came in. "The governors are calling us to a meeting. If you could meet me in the surveillance room, that would be wonderful."

While the screens in the surveillance room were intended to watch the feeds from our drones, they doubled as our means of communication during video meetings whenever they were called. Ava had spent several hours setting up the video calling system in our base and for the governors.

"It's good to speak to you all again," Lawrence said as the call connected. "Of course, Margaret and Sylvestor are in attendance, along with Marie White, Goldheart's governor, who has been recovering from the injuries she sustained during her escape to the Opposition States."

Marie gave a slight wave. "Hello there! It's wonderful to finally speak to all of you."

"Likewise," I replied. "We've been defending Goldheart against RA forces. Swindance is currently the most at-risk Opposition holding in the state. Information received from a spy on our side told us that Krisprelli would be sending more of his men there in the coming days."

Ava and Samuel were working to get the drone feeds back up on another set of screens, leaving Freya and I to do the talking during the meeting. For the most part, the meeting went on without many things of significant importance being discussed. We ensured that every Opposition state other than Goldheart was still secure and discussed future plans, with Freya taking the lead in discussions for some time.

"I heard you were injured in Frostmorden. How are you recovering?" Marie asked Freya. It was obvious she actually cared about Freya's response.

"It's not too painful for me, but I'll need to be careful as I heal. I'm only able to walk around right now due to an apparatus Ava built for me."

"I hope you're able to make a quick recovery from your injuries. I appreciate your help in fighting Krisprelli."

"Thank you, ma'am."

"I believe we can conclude this meeting now," Sylvestor spoke up suddenly, "unless there are any last-minute additions that need to be discussed."

Freya and I concluded that we had nothing further to discuss, as did the governors, and thus our meeting concluded. Ava and Samuel had been watching the drone feeds for the past hour during the meeting, but the feeds didn't show anything major happening. As the meeting concluded, the screen that Freya and I had been using to talk with the governors flipped back to the drone's video feed. We all stayed in the surveillance room to watch it in the event the RA forces were marching on Swindance.

Samuel spoke up after some time. "Do you think it'll happen today?"

"The letter from Fredric said within the next three days. Assuming that included yesterday, if they don't attack today, it will happen tomorrow for sure," I replied.

We continued to watch the monitors for the next several hours until the sun had nearly set. Finally, we saw it: several RA troops marching toward Swindance. We radioed the troops deployed to the city and ordered them to open fire. Shortly after, we saw our soldiers shooting down the RA forces. What we did not expect, however, was an RA soldier getting close enough to plant and set off a bomb.

Twenty of our Opposition soldiers died in the blast, and even more were injured. Those who had not been caught in the blast continued fighting until they had taken the life of every person they could see who was wearing a Royal Army insignia. The medics worked to treat the injured as quickly as they could, but there were simply too many injuries for them to deal with.

Freya spoke, quite shaken by what just occurred. "Order them to bring the injured back here. We'll send a truck to carry them back. Once we bring in the injured, the uninjured troops who brought them will return to Swindance. We'll have another truck carry the dead back here for burial."

I radioed the troops, ordering them to carry the injured back to the base, dispatching a vehicle to retrieve them on their way. I then dispatched another vehicle and ordered it to drive directly to Swindance to recover the dead. We would need to keep as many of our soldiers there as possible in case of further RA advancements. Krisprelli would keep the pressure on us for as long as he could.

We kept watch of the video feeds, making sure Thompsonville and Frostmorden weren't also attacked. Once the injured arrived, we helped carry them to the medical ward, where Ava began working on them with the help of our other medical technicians. After keeping contact with our troops still on the battlefield for several more hours, we finally became too exhausted to continue. I had nearly fallen asleep in the surveillance room before Samuel decided we all needed to rest. Ava continued working in the ward, treating injuries, while Samuel and I headed to our rooms to rest as much as we could. I noticed, however, that Samuel didn't actually enter his room. Instead, he turned and left, and I was too tired to call after him.

The fact that only 20 lost their lives seemed like a small gift. Perhaps we had sated Mortality's bloodlust enough through killing Krisprelli's troops that it did not wish to devour too greedily on our side. Even then, however, 20 people losing their lives were still too many. I drifted into unconsciousness while thinking of how much higher that number would rise.

CHAPTER SEVEN

The next day, we attended a funeral service for the Opposition members who had been killed by the bomb the day before. They had been buried during the early morning, and the service was held for all of them together. Cassius Coville, the governor of the Opposition state of Yellowbend, came to Esterden to speak at the funeral and act as the priest. It was a quiet, somber affair as we paid our respects to those who had died for us. How regular would this event become?

I walked through the cemetery, looking at the newly dug graves and gravestones being made quickly but with enough care to still be respectful to the dead. They had little more than the names of the dead engraved on them, along with small, decorative designs around the names. I knew little about those who had died in the battle, and I did not even recognize the names on some of the gravestones. It was hard for me to realize that everyone who had been buried knew quite well who I was and respected me, while I knew little, if anything, of them. To them, I was a leader, someone they respected. To me, I knew them only as mere members of our group. I continued along my train of thought until Samuel began walking beside me and started to speak.

THE WAR OF WALNEYRIA

"Day by day, this cemetery continues to grow fuller with the bodies of our people. Did you know any of them?" Samuel spoke quietly, with a mournful tone.

"I recognized the names of half of them, but the others were not names I had come to recognize since our war began."

"Freya knew them all by name. She already returned to base; she was starting to get weak."

"It doesn't surprise me that she'd know all of them," I said. "She has always cared greatly for those fighting for us."

"They gave their lives for us, and they'll never know if we were able to bring about the change they died for. We should all fight even harder so they won't have died for nothing."

"Once we take Goldheart, we'll begin to march even farther into Krisprelli's territory," I assured him. "In time, we'll make him pay for what he's done to Walneyria. His death won't bring back those we've lost, but it shall be retribution for Walneyria."

"How backward it seems that to prevent bloodshed, we have to inflict bloodshed of our own."

"The blood we spill is from the guilty to stop them from tainting the soil with innocent blood."

"And shall we be considered innocent, Nate?" He seemed desperate for an answer—strange since Samuel rarely sought my counsel and was several years older than me. He would have everyone assume we were beneath him.

"Innocence is determined by the jury you are placed against," I answered as best I could. "To Walneyria, we are guilty; to the Opposition, we are innocent and fighting to save those who have done no wrong."

Samuel turned away from me without saying another word. He walked through the cemetery as I began to walk back toward our base. Samuel had questioned our actions since the beginning, and we had carried on several debates of right and wrong. While I knew he would not go against the Opposition, his increasingly skeptical personality had begun to concern me. I set aside my concern as I made my way to the base.

Once I had made my way inside, I checked on Freya, now resting inside her own room rather than in the medical ward. A small tablet computer with a map of Walneyria containing intricately drawn battle plans was on her bedside table. Knowing Freya, she had been working on those plans for several days, likely even before her injury. Most of what she had planned was for taking control of Goldheart, but she had also drawn up strategies for what we'd do afterward. I set the tablet down carefully and left the room.

Samuel was in the office, but due to our earlier discussion, I decided it was better to leave him to himself for now. Ava was in her workshop, tinkering with various bits and bobs of scavenged technology and metal. I walked into the workshop and sat down. Ava noticed me as I walked in but continued to work for a few more minutes on whatever she was making.

"I've not had many resources for my work since the war began," Ava said finally, still working on what she was building, "but I've been able to make do with what we have."

"How did you build those legs for Freya, then? They seemed rather advanced."

"In truth, I had already built the basic structure and metallic plates that held the various technical pieces of the apparatus, as well as the neural connection port. I just made the last few adjustments to it after Freya was injured. I had originally intended to use the device for my father so he would be able to walk again; but as you know, my dreams of being able to do so were taken from me."

"We'll make Krisprelli pay for what he's done. Everyone he's taken from us will be at peace when we get to him."

"I do not seek revenge in the death of Krisprelli. But his death means freedom for those still alive," she said. "We mourn who we've lost and let their deaths fuel our spirit, but the revenge of taking

Krisprelli's life is only a small fragment of joy that can be devoured in an instant by the negativity of our world."

"Once we've taken the last breath from Krisprelli's body, we can end this war, take Walneyria into our hands, and lead people to a new prosperity where everyone will be free. Our loved ones will be proud of our accomplishments then, don't you think?"

"I'm sure they'll be very proud of us killing dozens of people, yes."

"I didn't . . . "

"Nate, we can drop this conversation, or you can leave my workshop. Personally, I'm fine with either choice."

I took the hint and switched to a different topic. "What are you working on there?"

"I'm testing a ballistics-resistant material that will be stronger than our current armor." Her voice became more confident and light. "If I can work out how to easily create and produce it in large quantities, I can reinforce our troops' armor and minimize our casualties on the field."

"Have you made any advances in terms of treating injuries?"

"I've been working on synthesizing new medicines to speed along the healing process, but it's been slow work with what I have here. I'm hoping I'll get access to more proper equipment from Goldheart once we've rid the state of the Royal Army."

"That won't be long from now," Freya said excitedly as she rushed into the room. "We received another letter from Fredric. Krisprelli is sending a large group of his forces into Goldheart as a last stand. If we can repel his attack, the state will be in our control."

Ava turned away from what she was working on to face Freya. "And if we lose this battle, he'll take Goldheart and continue to march into our territory until he's killed all of us. This is a gambit we can't stand to lose."

"I've sent as many of our troops to Goldheart as I possibly can while still leaving enough at base for defense, if needed. After today, Goldheart will be in Opposition control."

"Or," I spoke up, "we'll lose almost every able-bodied fighter we have, allowing Krisprelli's forces to march into our holdings, essentially unopposed. We face an unimaginable risk for a relatively small reward."

"We'll have more resources and people for our cause. That's not a minor reward!"

"Freya," Ava spoke up again, "everyone in Swindance, Thompsonville, and Frostmorden already evacuated to the Opposition when the RA took over the towns. There's little population spread across the remaining area of Goldheart. The additional resources would be rather welcome, however."

Ava turned back to her work, and Freya looked rather disappointed that Ava and I doubted her plan to send so many of our people to their deaths for the defense of a single state. It was a fact that Goldheart was an excellent strategic holding for the Opposition, even if they had not declared their loyalty in name. The state had acted as a buffer between Krisprelli's Walneyria and the Opposition States and afforded us several potential paths into Walneyria to face Krisprelli's forces. If this battle went in our favor, we could exercise our power in the region and once again hold strategic paths into the lands that Krisprelli holds. Freya had surely already created plans for what we would do to utilize those paths.

I left the workshop as Ava continued her work in relative silence. I went to the surveillance room, where I assumed Freya had gone so she would have a view of the fighting once it began. As I expected, Freya was sitting in front of the largest screens in the room, each one showing different camera feeds—one in Thompsonville, another in Swindance, and the third in Frostmorden. The other screens showed views of various parts of Goldheart. On every screen, I saw dozens of our soldiers standing vigilantly, watching for RA troops. How many of the people on these screens would live to see tomorrow?

I began to receive the answer to that much sooner than I had expected. Royal Army soldiers suddenly shot down several of our soldiers, and I counted at least two dozen dead with many more injured. I watched the events with Freya for some time until Ava and Samuel joined us. Various Opposition members continued to enter the room as we watched the fighting progress.

For hours, we watched as several people, both from our side and Krisprelli's, were injured and killed. Several more hours passed until we received a radio transmission from one of our soldiers in Swindance, telling us they had killed every Royal Army soldier they had encountered. In time, we received transmissions from Frostmorden and Thompsonville to tell us of their victory. The other groups of soldiers Freya had dispatched reported the same. We had numerous casualties of our own in the fighting, but Goldheart was now firmly in Opposition control.

Ava stood and turned toward Freya. "All things considered, the outcome could have been much worse. Your gamble paid off for us in the end."

Freya spoke as she rose steadily from her seat. "Tomorrow, we'll begin recovering materials and resources from Goldheart. Tonight, we order our troops back to base for a well-deserved rest. We'll send several vehicles to pick them up, along with the injured and dead."

She radioed to the various groups of soldiers deployed in Goldheart, ordering them to wait in their positions until they were picked up and to group together the injured and dead in the meantime. Ava returned to her workshop, and Samuel went back to his office. Freya and I remained in the surveillance room with the other Opposition members who had not left. We all had different conversations for some time while our people were being retrieved from Goldheart. As they returned, we helped the injured to the medical ward and gave them basic treatment until Ava came in to give them full examinations and treatment.

I helped bury the dead, recording their names and grave placements for when their gravestones would be made. More came to aid us in the burial. After several hours, we had buried everyone we had lost. Would they have a funeral as the others, or would we simply move on to tomorrow, barely mourning them? So many of us had already been lost, and we could barely afford further losses. How much longer would our bloodshed continue?

I spent another night lying in bed and asking myself those questions, the same questions I'd been asking myself since this all began. Was our fighting worth the losses we suffered? Would we see the end we fought for? Or was our fighting in vain, prolonging the march to our deaths? I let the questions echo through my mind as sleep swept over my body.

CHAPTER EIGHT

W e held another funeral the next morning, this time attended by Lawrence, Margaret, Sylvestor, Marie, and Cassius—every Opposition governor I had personally met. They all gave brief speeches, showing their respect and gratitude for those we had lost. Cassius once again acted as priest for the funeral, performing the religious aspect of the ceremony for those who believed. Sylvestor, Marie, and Cassius remained in Esterden for the day, while Lawrence and Margaret needed to return to Highborough. They walked with me while Freya, Ava, and Samuel hurried back to the surveillance room.

Marie stepped toward me and offered a light hug. "I must thank you for bringing Goldheart into Opposition control. Knowing my people are safe from Krisprelli's regime helps me rest easier."

"I'm not the one you should thank. I did little when it came to the fighting in the state. Our soldiers, the living and dead, deserve every bit of praise. Freya, too. Without her planning, we would not have been able to defend the state as well as we did."

"Nate," Cassius said as he walked toward Marie and me, "we haven't had the opportunity to talk with each other properly yet."

"I'll be on my way, then." Marie excused herself to allow Cassius and me to talk with each other.

Cassius seemed upset by Marie's leaving but continued. "How did you come to found the Opposition with the others?"

"I saw my parents and brother killed in front of me. Ava had been a friend for some time before the Opposition formed, and she had lost her father to the regime, giving us both a motive for rebellion. We worked together to establish an underground resistance force and were soon joined by Freya and Samuel."

"And who had they lost? What led them to join you?"

"Freya lost her wife, and Samuel's son was taken by Krisprelli, but they imprisoned him rather than killing him outright."

"Samuel has the chance to retrieve what was taken from him. So many of us would do anything to afford such an opportunity . . . " Cassius's voice trailed.

"Samuel is a good man—if not paranoid at times—but he's done many good things to advance the Opposition's influence."

"And he's performed an excellent job in doing so," Sylvestor said, joining our discussion. "If it weren't for him, the Opposition almost definitely would not have grown as quickly or as large as it has."

"His work in furthering the Opposition has been truly impressive. Let us hope it will continue," I agreed.

"Well, Nate," Sylvestor spoke once more, "I believe we've gotten to the point where words are not enough for our battles. We're well past the time for action, considering how hard-fought the battle for Goldheart was. Fighting in states where the Opposition hasn't already taken hold will be much more difficult for us."

I chose my next words carefully because of Sylvestor. "I agree with you, but I am sure that Freya is putting together battle plans as we speak. She has an incredible tactical skill."

"Shall we go to your base, then? We can see her plans firsthand!" Cassius spoke with great enthusiasm.

Sylvestor, Cassius, and I walked back to the base together. Marie had already made her way there while Cassius and I were talking, and Ava, Freya, Samuel, and Marie were all gathered in Freya's planning room. She had laid a large map of Walneyria on the table. It included detailed sketches of plans, troop placements, scouting times, and paths for troops to take. Sylvestor, Cassius, and I all sat down and listened to Freya's explanation of the plans.

"Our soldiers," she began, "will take paths from Goldheart into the states of Hampkurth and Wealdsey. These states are still under Krisprelli's control, but we can weaken his hold and eventually bring the states into the Opposition. Every state we take from him brings us yet closer to ending his reign once and for all."

Sylvestor stood from his seat and closely examined the plans. "The fighting in these states won't be as easy as it was for us in Goldheart where we already had a slight hold of the region. These states are quite firmly in Krisprelli's hands."

"That may be true," Freya began her reply, "but if we do not keep fighting, we will never free our country from the damnable regime of Krisprelli."

"And how many more people can we stand to lose?" Sylvestor yelled.

"I understand we've lost several people, Sylvestor, but we must fight until we cannot any longer."

"And shall that be when our last soldier draws his last breath as the Royal Army marches into our territory?"

"It shall be whenever I decide it shall be, Sylvestor."

"And who gives you the authority?" Sylvestor's face was red.

"I've only ever calculated the best routes for our soldiers. If you doubt my allegiance or my abilities, you can leave this room."

"What did you just say to me?"

"Leave this room. Now!"

"What authority do you have to—"

"You govern a single state. I am a founding member of our organization. Your state may hold our capital, but Nate is our president. Now leave!" Freya pointed toward the door.

"Nate." Sylvestor turned to me. "What do you have to say of this?"

"Freya asked you to leave, and I order you to do so."

Sylvestor left the room, quite visibly upset. I was concerned about what he might say to the others but assumed it would be okay overall since Marie and Cassius had seen the entire exchange. Sylvestor had become increasingly desperate to cling to the power he held as time went on, as if it would be taken from him during the war. Freya returned to detailing her plans once Sylvestor had left.

"Wealdsey would present an easier fight for us than Hampkurth due to a smaller number of RA forces in the area, while Hampkurth would allow us further tactical openings, along with several more potential resources. I believe that fighting to take Wealdsey would be a more logical decision for us with our shrinking number of troops."

Ava stood up and handed a stack of papers to Freya. "I've been researching methods to create a material that would make our armor much more resistant to enemy bullets. I've also devised methods to increase the effectiveness of our field medicine, but I lack the resources and equipment to make the final touches on both. If I have time to get my hands on what I need and finish the tests, we would be much more well equipped for battle before we go farther into enemy territory."

"And where would you be able to get what you need?" Freya asked.

"I mostly need equipment, machinery, and the like—all of it in Goldheart. The last few resources I need could likely be found in Goldheart as well."

"Well, then," I said, "let's go to Goldheart."

Ava and Freya were pleased by how ready I was to go, while Samuel was his usual uninterested self. Cassius and Marie said they needed to find Sylvestor, so they could not come with us. Freya got a group of various people from around the base to help us, and we split into three teams, one team for each major town. We kept radios and cameras on us to communicate with one another and share what we found during the search.

After we searched for a few hours, we were able to find nearly everything Ava needed. We found all the various machines she would need, along with the parts needed to repair them, but we had yet to find some of the resources she needed. After several more hours of searching, including searches in the smaller areas of Goldheart, we finally found the right supplies. We returned to Esterden, carefully carrying what we had recovered.

We brought everything into Ava's workshop, and she almost immediately began putting the various machines into their places and organizing the bits and bobs we had found. Her worktable was scattered with what we brought back, along with the work she had already been able to complete. With what she had now, Ava would hopefully be able to create stronger armor to better protect our soldiers and better medicine to treat them if they were injured.

"What is the material you're creating for the armor?" Freya asked Ava as she set a box of materials down.

"A thicker plating using a stronger alloy with a gravity field generated around the armor. If I can make it work properly, it will greatly increase the protection our armor provides."

I inspected the various machines around the workshop before I asked, "What would the gravity field do?"

"In theory, it would work to catch the bullet and greatly slow down its speed. I likely won't be able to make it strong enough to slow the bullets down completely, but it should slow them down enough for their damage to be quite minor."

"And the new medicines—what will they do?"

"Better pain killers, for a start. If I can synthesize them properly, I'll be able to create something to speed up the healing process. The equipment we recovered today will be a great help, but it's still a rather primitive setup when it comes to what I'm attempting to create with it. Nevertheless, we're making wonderful progress here, Nate."

"Perhaps," Freya began, "once we've taken more states, we'll have access to a more proper setup for your work."

"That would be rather wonderful, but what we retrieved today is serviceable for now. However, I could work better if it were a bit quieter in here." Ava shot each of us a look.

Freya and I sheepishly left Ava's workshop to allow her to work in peace. Freya returned to her room to rest since movement had become a strain for her. I returned to my room and grabbed a book from my shelf, not paying any particular attention to which one I had grabbed. I ended up with *The History of Walneyria* and sat at my desk to read. It proved to be an enjoyable enough way to pass time for a few hours until Ava came to my room to pull me to her workshop. Once I got there, I saw she had brought Samuel and Freya as well.

Samuel crossed his arms and asked, "Why did you drag us to your workshop this time, Ava?"

Ava didn't respond immediately but moved an armor stand into view that had a modified armor chest piece on it. She pressed a button on the shoulder plate of the armor, which caused a blue, somewhat glowing aura to appear around the armor. She then took a pistol and fired at the armor stand. To our astonishment, the bullet slowed down almost entirely, leaving only the slightest scratch on the armor's plating.

Ava turned the armor off and set the pistol down. "The gravity field works exactly as I expected. I won't have enough resources to fit every suit of armor with the gravity field, but I should have enough to at least reinforce them using the alloy I created."

"And the medicine?" I asked. "How is progress on it?"

"I was able to make small doses of the painkillers. I gave them to the more seriously injured patients in the medical ward. The drug to speed the healing process will take more time; it's quite an advanced project and needs precise measurements and incredible care. I'll continue my research on it once I finish the work on our armor. You can all go back to what you were doing."

We left the room as Ava fiddled around with the armor. She was an incredibly intelligent, talented woman, but she got ahead of herself at times. Her research into advancement for our armor was indisputably incredible and would definitely cut down on the number of soldiers injured or killed in battle. If she was able to synthesize and produce the medicine that would increase the rate of healing, we would not need to wait as long for our injured to recover before they could fight again. This war was terrible for everyone, but the technological advancements we would make because of it would be incredible.

Ava's work would prevent further deaths. It would anger Mortality, because we would be depriving it of its food. Had we not already fed it enough since this war began? It had had a feast of souls, yet it yearned to feast even more. Perhaps if we starved it enough, it would die, and we would be safe from its hungry, twisted claws.

The senators who joined us for the funeral today had already returned to Highborough. I was sure that the next time we spoke, Sylvestor would be pleasant, and I was sure Freya would continue to work on her plans to infiltrate Hampkurth and Wealdsey in order to further weaken Krisprelli's hold of Walneyria. In time, Walneyria would belong to the people once again. We would fight to make it so.

CHAPTER NINE

My sleep became more restless as the days progressed, plaguing me with violent hallucinations. Would I sleep peacefully once this war ended, or would I continue to see those I cared for get killed in my dreams? How much more bloodshed would we endure before we could declare peace for our nation? I rose slowly from my bed, still pondering how long it might be until I could get the answers to my questions. No sooner had I gotten out of bed than Ava came to pull me to her workshop once again.

"What is it this time, Ava?"

"I modified your armor, specifically for you. I think you'll appreciate what I changed."

Ava presented me with a suit of armor. Outwardly, its appearance was scarcely different from the standard armor we were using. The plating appeared slightly more bulky because of the thicker material Ava had built into it, and the gravity field generators could be seen across the structure of the armor. Additionally, the forearm of the left bracer was larger than the right.

"How exactly have you modified it for me?"

"It has the gravity wells built in, something I was only able to build into a handful of our armor. Additionally, I attached the thicker plating to it and built the gauntlet blade into it. Now you can be reckless with a much smaller chance of dying than before."

I put the armor on to test its maneuverability. The gauntlet blade activated the same way it had before, but it was noticeably more fluid in its extension. Ava pulled down a panel on the arm, revealing a button. She pressed it and then slid the panel back into place. The button was the activator for the gravity wells that built the gravity fields around the suit. Although the glow from the field was less noticeable than it was when Ava showed it to us before, the effect was not at all diminished.

Ava returned to work on another suit of armor. "I've fitted 13 of our suits of armor with the gravity wells; that's all I had resources for. I also fitted most of the suits with the better plating, but I'll need more time to finish all of them."

"And the medicine?"

"I made some progress on the formula, but synthesizing and creating doses will take more time."

"I'll let you continue with your work, then."

Carefully taking off the armor, I put it back on its stand and then walked throughout the base for a while, talking with various Opposition members. Freya was still drafting tactics for our future movements, so I chose not to disturb her. Realizing I had not had a private conversation with Samuel in some time, I decided it might be good to do so and made my way to his office where he was writing in a thick, leather-bound notebook.

Samuel turned his head toward me as I walked inside. "What do you need, Nate?"

"It's been a few days since we spoke privately. Don't you think it would be good to do so?"

"What do you have to discuss that needs to be said in private? Private conversations seem a waste for nonprivate matters."

"What is it you're writing in that book?"

"Nothing of your concern, Nate. Certain private matters are best kept private, even during one-on-one conversations."

"Okay, then. Is there anything you would like to talk about?"

"As a matter of fact, there is! There's been quite an annoying pest bothering me recently. His name is Nate. Now get out of my office."

I said nothing to Samuel as I left. What had caused him to be so cross with me? I didn't believe I'd said anything wrong, but Samuel had always been quicker to anger than the others. I was curious what he was writing that he wanted to keep private, but I would not pry into it since I did not wish to anger Samuel more than I already had. I decided to talk with Freya and discuss what plans she had created.

"Hello there, Nate," Freya said as I entered the room. "Good to see you."

"Hey, Freya, how are the plans coming along?"

"I've made strategies and tactical plans for infiltrating Wealdsey. If we focus on taking Wealdsey first, we'll have more ways to get into Hampkurth when we're ready to do so."

"And the governors of those states, do you know if they're in support of the Opposition?" I asked nervously.

"Wealdsey's governor, Aleksei Krobic, is in support of the Opposition," Freya explained. "However, the governor of Hampkurth, Zoe Korenz, is a supporter of Krisprelli."

"Where is Aleksei now? If he's still in Wealdsey, he's in danger."

"He's in Wealdsey, but he's sent letters to us via our underground couriers to tell us of his support," Freya said. "We'll be sure to get him into the Opposition States as soon as possible."

"And Korenz? Where is she?"

"She's in Hampkurth. I do not wish to kill her, however. We would have a valuable bargaining chip if we were to capture her alive."

"You raise an excellent point," I said, "but how far could we really get with a bargaining chip and diplomacy against Krisprelli's regime? If we attempted to approach him nonviolently, he would have his soldiers shoot us down immediately."

"It will be good for us to have the opportunity nonetheless, Nate. If nothing else, she could give us information to aid in our fight against the regime."

"All good points. What is our immediate plan of action, then?"

"First, we wait until Ava has finished the modifications on our armor and has created the new medicine she's been synthesizing. Once those are complete, we'll begin our march into Wealdsey, rescue Krobic, and begin to remove the Royal Army forces from the state. Once that's done, we'll gather any resources and machinery we can find from the state for Ava to use in her work, allow the recovery of our wounded, and prepare to march into Hampkurth."

"How heavily defended is Wealdsey?"

"It's more heavily guarded than Goldheart was but overall still lighter in defenses than other areas in Walneyria. Taking the state won't deal a heavy blow to Krisprelli's power, but it will be a blow nonetheless."

"Any blow we can deal to his control will be a gain for the Opposition."

"I need more time to work on these plans, Nate. I don't mean to be rude, but could you give me some time alone?"

"Of course, Freya. Your planning is vital to our success."

I went back to walking around the base since I had little else to do. I saw Samuel leave his office carrying the notebook he had been writing in, but he walked the other way as if avoiding any interaction with me. What was Samuel trying to hide?

I went back to my room and sat at my desk, passing the time by sketching in notebooks and reading some small books I had. Time's progression seemed to slow down in recent days, perhaps due to the relative calm after we took Goldheart. Whatever the cause, it had been a pleasant feeling to not have to bury anyone else for some time. Ava had spent a large portion of the day working on our armor, but she once again came to my room to ask me to her workshop.

"I finished the armor modifications," Ava said, "so I started working on the synthesis of the new medication. I perfected the formula and process of manufacturing doses and just need to test it."

"Okay. What do you need me to do?" I asked, confused.

Ava pulled out a small knife and lightly grabbed my wrist. "I'll just make a small cut on your finger and drip some of the medication on it."

I reluctantly allowed Ava to cut my finger. After doing so quickly, she picked up a vial delicately, taking a pipette containing the light green liquid out of the bottle. She squeezed a few drops of the drug onto my finger, and the bleeding stopped quickly, along with the pain.

"It won't instantly heal wounds," Ava said after she put the medicine on the cut, "but it will tremendously increase the rate that the body heals wounds. Our injured will be able to return to battle much more quickly once I've produced enough of the drug."

"Will you give some of this to Freya to aid in her recovery?"

"She already told me she didn't want any of it; she'd rather our soldiers receive it. Freya's also already far enough along in the healing process that the drug would do little to speed it along. It's meant to be administered within a few days of sustaining injuries. It would still have a minor effect after that timeframe, but healing would not be significant enough to justify using the small supply we have."

"How much time do you think it will take you to produce a larger supply of it?"

"If I can work on refining the process of manufacturing it, I could have a larger supply ready by tomorrow. I understand we can't afford to spend much more time waiting to resume fighting."

"Freya is still working on refining her plans, and she wants us to be as prepared as possible before we go into battle once again," I said.

"The more time we spend not fighting, the more time Krisprelli has to bolster his numbers and send them around the country. We need to keep fighting him as often as possible, so I will create as much of this medicine in as short a time as possible."

"Well put, Ava. Is there anything I can help you with?"

"I can finish this on my own, but I thank you for the offer."

Ava turned toward the machines she had set up for the process of creating the medicine. The rate at which she worked was truly impressive. I looked around the base for Samuel but could not find where he had gone. His secrecy and temperament concerned me, but I figured there was little reason to allow it to worry me.

I returned to my room and sat at my desk to write in one of the notebooks I had accumulated, getting out several thoughts and ideas as they came to mind. Perhaps once this war ended, I could sit down and write a cohesive book rather than a randomly assembled collection of my thoughts, but it seemed little good in the present to muse about the actions of my future self. What if I did not even live to see that future?

I tried not to think about Samuel's actions from earlier in the day, but they still made me worry. It was likely this worry was unfounded, but I could not shake the feeling that perhaps Samuel was plotting something dreadful. I tried to steady and reassure myself that Samuel was one of our own and that we could trust him as a member of our group.

For the remainder of the day, I spent a large portion in my room, reading, writing, and sketching to pass the time. We would have only a handful more of peaceful days such as this until this war ended, but knowing that did not stop us from enjoying them whenever we were fortunate enough for them to happen. Once I had grown bored of the limited activities I had available to me, I left my room and went back to Ava's workshop to see her progress.

There were several vials on a table in the room, each filled with the medicine. It had appeared that Ava mostly automated the process of manufacturing the medication and only needed to remove the bottles from the line and attach the lids to them once they were full. I counted 28 vials on the table and watched as more filled up in front of me.

Ava was capping a vial as she spoke. "I spent quite some time modifying the machines and assembly line to automate it like this. Automating it also increased the amount I can produce by quite a sizable margin."

"That is wonderful, Ava! We should be able to treat quite a few people with this amount of medicine. Have you thought of a name for the drug?"

"*Sanitatem Celer.* It's Latin for "speedy healing." Not the most creative name, but it's still a name."

"Where'd you learn everything you know, anyway? You've never told me before."

Ava looked somewhat confused by the sudden question but offered an answer. "My father taught me mechanical and engineering skills when I was younger. I went to medical school for the medical knowledge and afterward attended school for engineering."

"That's a rather impressive amount of schooling. What motivated you to go through all of it?"

"I went to medical school to help my father when his health began to fail him and engineering school mostly for fun. It also helped that I would have the education to fix things when I needed to. That's much cheaper in the long run than paying a repair person every time something breaks." Ava smiled as she said that last sentence.

"I assume, then, that you attended school before you came to Walneyria?"

"Yes, that's correct. My father and I wanted to move to Walneyria after my mother died, but I was still going to school at that time, so we did not move until I graduated. I never anticipated I would use my education in the ways I have, though."

"You've been able to help so many people here. Your contributions to the Opposition will go on to help so many more people, Ava."

"I just hope I'll see the end of this war so I can continue to make advancements in a country at peace."

Ava returned to capping the vials of Sanitatem, but I could tell she was only doing it to keep her mind occupied. This war drained our energy and spirit from us, and we were constantly concerned with thoughts of whether we would live to see the end of it. I left Ava's workshop so she could have some time to herself. Her work was incredible, but the reason she had made so many wonderful advancements was rather grim. I returned to my room for rest.

For the first night in a long series of nights, my mind was relatively unburdened with thoughts of death. I was not at complete ease, but I enjoyed the relative calm. I lay down that night, not thinking of the dreadful things I had seen but rather about the positive things and about the future. Ava's medical advances would be wonderful for treating the sick once the war was over and when she could properly manufacture it in larger quantities. We would free this nation and its people from the rule of a tyrant. We could live safely and happily and begin to recover. We would pay our respects to those we lost, and we would live the rest of our lives for them. I could not wait to see that day.

CHAPTER TEN

I woke up easily and quickly the next morning, my brain not tormented with nightmares and hallucinations as it had grown pleasure in doing. I was sure this would be the last morning for some time when I had the luxury of waking peacefully. Ava had left my suit of armor on a stand in my room with a note attached to it that said I might need it. Perhaps we would be returning to battle sooner than I had anticipated. I left my room to find Freya, who was in her planning room as I had expected.

"The Wealdsey plans are almost complete," Freya said to me without moving from her maps, "and I've begun drawing up plans for Hampkurth. I'll need to prepare plans for two fronts—one for attacking from Wealdsey and another for attacking from here."

"And a good morning to you, too, Freya."

"Ah, yes, good morning, Nate. My perception of time is a bit off; I've been working quite late to make these plans."

"And by late, you mean the entire night?"

"You can see right through me," Freya said, smiling.

"It is good to hear that the strategies are coming along as needed, however. When do you expect we'll be ready to fight?"

"Potentially today, but tomorrow would be a more likely—and safe—bet. It will give me time to iron out the finer details and potential gaps in the plans I've drawn up. I'll make sure we can resume fighting as quickly as possible. We need to deprive Krisprelli's forces of as much time as possible to prepare against us."

"I definitely agree. If we keep giving time for the Royal Army to plot and prepare against us, we'll have a much more difficult time when it comes to fighting them."

"Indeed." She kept her eyes on her work. "We need to prepare our soldiers to return to battle and get everything else ready while we're preparing. Armor, medical kits, weapons, plans, everything. We'll bring the fight to Wealdsey, we'll take down more of Krisprelli's soldiers, and we will continue the fight for the prosperity of this country because it's the only option we have."

"This nation will be ours once again, Freya. The people we've lost, the people who were taken from us—we can't bring them back, but we can fight in their spirit to save others from suffering their fate."

"I will see to it personally that Krisprelli burns for the pain he's inflicted on the people of Walneyria. He's murdered our family, our friends, and the people we loved. He deserves everything he will receive for his crimes against this nation."

"Once we've made our way to Krisprelli, let us all take a stab at him, literally."

"That is a wonderful idea, but one that will take a rather long path to get to. For now, I should continue evaluating these plans. A bit of quiet, please?"

I left the room at Freya's request and walked about the halls thinking about various things. How long would the path to Krisprelli be until we made it to the end? How many more lives would be taken as we made our way along that path? Would those I had come closest to live to see the end of our path? So many questions, each of them lacking an answer.

I looked around for Samuel but was unable to find him anywhere around the base. That worried me. Had he begun actively avoiding me? I kept walking around the base, trying to occupy myself and think little of my concerns. I had small conversations with several Opposition members, ate a small meal, and exercised for a few minutes. I'd used up almost every way I had available to pass the time, so I went to Ava's workshop to see how many more vials of the Sanitatem Celer she had produced.

Ava was capping a bottle of the medicine, but the machinery that had been producing it was turned off. A table in the workshop was covered from end to end with bottles of the drug. We would have enough to treat several people for a decent while, even if we were unable to make more. Ava put the lid on the last vial and began packing them into a box with care. I did not disturb her until she had packed every bottle and placed the box back on the table.

"That's the last bottle," Ava said as she stood up from her seat. "We don't have enough of the ingredients to produce more right now. The amount we were able to produce is still a good supply, though. We'll be able to treat our people for quite some time."

I looked around at the machinery. "How much of a dose will every injured person need when we begin administering it?"

"It will depend on the seriousness of the injuries they've sustained, but I'd say that on average, we should get five dosages out of each vial, and anyone we give it to will only need one dose. The effect of the medicine doesn't dissipate until after a point where giving more doses would be an essential waste of the stuff."

"Even then, let's hope we don't end up having to use too much of it."

"Better for us to use all of it and lose no one than use little and lose everyone," I said.

"I agree with you entirely, but my point is that I hope the number of times we need to use the drug will be as minimal as possible. If you excuse me, I need to bring this to the medical ward." Ava picked up the box of Sanitatem and started carrying it to the ward. Her creation of the drug was impressive, but I hoped we would not have to use much of the surplus we had built up. Having the drug would be an incredible aid to the Opposition, but if we were to use such a large amount of the drug, it would just be a further reminder of the sheer numbers Krisprelli had against us and how easily his armies could inflict injuries on our people.

Samuel was still nowhere to be found. Perhaps my concern was unfounded, but I had a growing anxiety he was planning to do something. I shook the feeling and returned to my room for some time, writing in a journal and listening to music through an old turntable we had found in a forgotten storage building in Goldheart. The records that were stored with it weren't what I would normally choose, but it was still pleasant to have them, if only for the noise to make it feel less lonely on the base.

Freya sent a message through the comms station in my room to ask me to come to her planning room. I made my way there as quickly as I could. When I entered, I saw the same maps I had seen earlier, but the plans she had drawn on them were modified in several ways. The front lines were less spread out, and the divisions were larger but would infiltrate through fewer points to capture and hold more territory in less time.

Freya was leaning over a table that had a map spread across it. "I've finished the plans for Wealdsey. Whenever you're ready, we'll start getting the troops prepared and begin infiltrating the state."

"Let's begin the fighting tomorrow but tell our soldiers today. They need time to mentally prepare before we once more send them into battle."

"I agree. That is a good idea. We do not wish to send them into battle before they are prepared to do so."

"Shall I give them a speech to prepare them, then?"

"If you wish to do so, no one shall stop you. Nate, you've always had a certain grace about you when you speak."

"I appreciate that compliment, Freya. I'll go tell the troops now."

I began to walk out of the room until Freya spoke up, "Have you seen Samuel recently? I've been worried about him."

"I've been looking for him, but I haven't seen him. I tried to talk to him in his office the other day, but he seemed rather angry and yelled at me to get out. I saw him in the hall later that day, but he walked the other way as if to intentionally avoid me. Do you think he may be planning something?"

"I don't think he would be planning anything against us, but the fact that you've not been able to find him is concerning to me, especially considering his recent behavior. Once we find him, perhaps we should monitor him. We'd have to be careful that he didn't notice us doing so, however."

"If he were plotting something, don't you think being monitored would cause him to put a plan into motion more quickly if he were to find out?"

"Constant surveillance would be difficult," Freya said, "and he would definitely discover us if we were to attempt it. We'll need to watch him when he's near us and get other people on the base to monitor him whenever he's near them. Hopefully, we won't find anything unusual, but perhaps we will uncover a plot before he can spring it."

"Let's hope it is nothing and we are simply being paranoid for no good reason."

"Indeed. Now, go give that speech to our people."

I left the planning room and went to the barracks. Every member of our fighting force slept near the barracks, their rooms containing alarms to order them to the barracks whenever they were needed. A few of the soldiers were sitting around at tables in the barracks, and I sat near a few of them to consider my words for a few minutes. Once I decided what I would say to them, I stood up and pressed the button to assemble them in the barracks. I began to speak as soon as they arrived.

"Soldiers, friends, fellow Opposition members. Tomorrow, you will once again return to battle, this time in Wealdsey. It shan't be an easy fight, but it is necessary for our goals. The fighting we do tomorrow contributes to a greater future for us and our descendants. The wounds we receive and the scars they become are the signs of strife, the signs of battle. They are the signs that will show that you fought to protect the nation you call home. And our fighting continues to bring us closer to Krisprelli's hold. When we can march on that hold, we will end this war and the life of the tyrant who took everything away from us. You fight for yourself, for us, and for Walneyria, and that fighting will not end until we have drawn out Krisprelli's last breath."

I received several cheers from the crowd, and everyone in the room seemed inspired by my words. I believed in every single word that left my mouth in those few short minutes. Everyone in the room wasn't fighting for any one person—they were fighting for a nation, for the country they called home, the country twisted by Krisprelli into what we were fighting. Everyone here would fight until they could not continue to fight. We all had our own personal reasons for why we fought, but we were all joined by a singular motive: the desire to free Walneyria, the desire for any friends and family they had been fortunate enough not to lose to live in peace. That was what we were all fighting for.

I spoke with several of them after I gave the speech. Some told me why they fought, the reason usually being the loss of loved ones to the regime. Others told me what they would do once the war was over, and others simply asked how my day was. It was a difficult time for everyone, but day to day, we made everything work, and we could convince ourselves for just a moment that it was like any regular day.

CHAPTER ELEVEN

We held some small festivities that night, drinking, storytelling, and relaxing with one another as if it was just another regular, unremarkable night. We knew that come tomorrow, some of the people in this room likely would not be with us any longer, but no one spoke of it. We needed to be able to have more nights like this. Freya and Ava eventually joined in on the activities with everyone else, and the night was generally carefree; that is, until Samuel walked into the room.

We did not approach him immediately, and he did not approach us. He went through the room and then out, likely to walk to his office. Freya and I had yet to bring up our concerns about Samuel to Ava, but it seemed she could tell something was the matter just by how our composures changed. We continued with the festivities of the night until everyone began to settle down and return to their rooms. I went back to my room, as well, and lay down on my bed.

Were we right to be concerned about Samuel? Where had he gone, and why had he returned so late as though trying to return when no one would see him? What was he planning that he was hiding from us? Perhaps he was plotting to aid us in our fight against Krisprelli. My anxieties did not allow me to entertain that idea for much longer, however.

I woke the next morning, my dreams bloodless but nevertheless anxiety-filled. Today would be the day we began the fight for Wealdsey, yet my concerns were focused on a matter of closer proximity. Samuel's sudden disappearance and reappearance had brought a great deal of concern to both Freya and me, but we had yet to talk to Ava about our concerns. My comms station had a light indicating a transmission was waiting to be read. It was from Freya, requesting me to come to the planning room, preferably out of sight of Samuel. I carefully made my way to the room, Samuel nowhere in sight.

Ava was already inside, and Freya made a motion for me to lock the door. I sat down in a chair adjacent to Ava. Freya had cleared off the table she had been using for planning and now set three cups of coffee on it. She sat on the chair across from me, drinking her coffee, and was quiet for a few minutes, likely while she thought of her words. After some time, she finally broke the silence.

"We need to keep an eye on Samuel. Whenever he is near us, we will watch him, but not in a way that would make it too obvious to him that we're doing so. We'll gather a small group of Opposition members and have them do the same. We can't keep a constant eye on him, but if we can keep a watch of his activities regularly enough, we can try to prevent anything he could be planning."

"And," Ava said in reply, "why have we begun to distrust Samuel? What has he done recently that warrants being suspicious of him?"

I collected my thoughts for a moment before I replied, "He's become more hostile and aggressive, not physically but in his speech and temper. It also seemed as if he were trying to stay away from me when I saw him in the hall a few days ago. Most importantly, however, he left the base without telling any of us, was gone for an entire day, and returned late in the night as if trying to avoid being seen."

"Hmm. I would agree that these are all valid points," Ava said thoughtfully. "What is it you're concerned he's doing?"

"There is nothing specific we're concerned about," Freya spoke once more, "but if he is planning anything, we need to stay vigilant and prevent any plans from taking hold. His position in our organization affords him several opportunities to act against us."

I considered the scale to which Samuel could turn people against us. If he had been plotting anything and had the time to get deep into a plan, he could bring several people into his fold to further his plans. If Samuel were against us, we had to assume there were others in our group who were helping advance his goals. If that were true, then how many people could we actually trust? Any questions I had today would not be answered until we had the answer to our question about Samuel.

"As for Wealdsey," Freya said, pulling out her map once again, "we'll have everyone prepare to leave, and as soon as they're all ready, we'll go. We'll distribute the other 12 pairs of gravity-field suits at random, and Nate already has his. Will you be fighting with them today, Nate?"

"Gladly. I've spent too much time here without the thrill of the fight."

Ava, Freya, and I returned to the barracks and gathered the soldiers. We drew names at random to decide who would receive one of the gravity suits. Once they were chosen, Ava demonstrated to them how to enable the field generators and stressed the importance of keeping them on during the fight. Ava made sure everyone was properly equipped with the necessary gear. Ava and Freya would stay behind to communicate with us and watch the battle from the drone feeds, as usual.

"Based on the video feeds,"—Ava's voice played through the helmet speakers—"Krisprelli has squads marching along the borders of Wealdsey, with dozens more holding the city of Lunarford. The fighting will be much more centrally focused than Goldheart."

"Understood. We've nearly made it to the infiltration point."

We were driven to Wealdsey rather than make the journey on foot since it was farther from our base than Goldheart. Several transports were carrying the divisions to the infiltration points Freya had designated. The plan was for smaller groups to take out the patrolling RA forces, while the main part of our forces, myself among them, would march toward Lunarford to challenge Krisprelli's hold.

We brought suppressed weaponry with us this time to take out any patrols we happened on before we made it to the city. We were able to shoot down any RA troops before they saw us, making the trek to Lunarford relatively easy. The snipers climbed to high ground and scanned for RA snipers as usual. I fired a shot from the suppressed pistol I had with me, taking out one soldier, and signaled our snipers to fire. It's the same way our battles had always begun. Ducking behind cover, I turned on my suit's gravity field since I had carelessly forgotten to do so.

We continued fighting the Royal Army forces, our snipers picking off some of them here and there, while our front-line forces laid down most of the fire. After numerous hours of combat, we had cleared a majority of the RA forces from the city while suffering only a few light injuries of our own and no deaths. The thicker armor had done its job to protect our people, and the gravity-field armor had done its job to slow down the bullets.

We made our way through Lunarford, clearing the remaining Royal Army forces from the city. The squads patrolling the border had made their way to the city to fight but were quickly taken out. After some time, the divisions we had sent specifically to take out the patrols joined us in the city. There were some injured and, unfortunately, one dead due to an exploding grenade.

Freya's voice came through the speakers: "The feeds aren't showing any more Royal Army members in the area. For now, we control the area. You should return to base and bring the injured and the dead with you."

Most of the injured were able to get themselves into the vehicles that picked us up, and I helped those who were unable to. We loaded the dead soldier into the vehicle, her armor damaged heavily by the grenade. The ride back to Esterden was unremarkable, and I made small talk with a few of the soldiers as we rode. Once we made it back, we helped the injured to the ward, and Ava distributed doses of Sanitatem to those who needed it. We buried the soldier who had been killed and quickly made her headstone. Though we could not give her a proper funeral, we paid our respects for a few minutes.

It had been a tiring day, but at least we had been fortunate enough to not lose a significant number of our own. We had taken Lunarford, but we could not say that Wealdsey was truly in our grasp. Our troops remained in the city to defend it from any further attacks by the regime's forces until we could be confident Krisprelli would cease attempts to keep control of the region.

I was going toward my room when Freya pulled me into her planning room once again. The tables and walls were bare, no longer with maps plastered on them, and Freya wore a grave expression on her face. Ava was already sitting at the table, and Freya paced around for some time until she finally sat down with us.

"Samuel's gone again," Ava said before Freya had the chance to. "Someone saw him leave this morning but did not approach him since they were concerned about what he might do."

I thought for a moment about that timeframe. "He would have had to leave early this morning, then. Perhaps even before our meeting? Why would he possibly leave that early?"

"Something secret," Freya said, offering her contribution to the discussion. "Something he could not allow anyone to find out about. Perhaps he had a meeting of his own."

"And who might he be meeting with that would need to be kept a secret?" Ava asked pointedly.

"I do not know if it was a meeting. I was simply suggesting that as a possibility."

"Ava does present a good question," I began. "If it was, in fact, a secret meeting, who might it have been with? If it was not a meeting, what other reason would he have for leaving the base so early and in secret?"

Ava was taking notes as she spoke. "We need to answer this question if at all possible. What was Samuel's reason for leaving that early?"

"It won't be possible for us to ask him directly," I replied. "There's no chance he would give us a factual answer. We would need to find any kind of clue from somewhere else."

"The doors to his office are locked; I already checked. We won't be able to find anything there," Ava said as she continued to take notes.

We continued discussions for several more minutes but were unable to come up with anything of value. Although entirely sure by this point that Samuel was up to something, we had no idea what it could be. The more time that passed with no answers, the more anxious we became. If his plans remained a mystery to us, we had no way to stop him before he could spring them into action and ensnare us in a trap. We would need to find any way possible to gain information on what Samuel was doing.

I returned to my room for some semblance of rest. Anything that would help restore my energy would be welcome, regardless of the dreams that came with it. Samuel's activities had become increasingly concerning, almost entirely because we did not know what those actions truly were. Samuel had become someone I had grown to call a friend, but was everything he had done for us a clever act to further some plot? Had we all been used as pawns for his scheme, willingly or otherwise? The anxiety caused by these questions helped prolong the time it took for exhaustion to carry me to sleep.

CHAPTER TWELVE

I was awakened by loud noises from the hall. Jumping out of bed, I opened my door slowly, trying to make as little noise as possible. What I saw when I opened the door was Samuel, running to his office. He had not seen me watching him and so did not stop. When I heard him lock the door of his office, I returned to my room and sent a message to Freya to tell her what I had just seen. She responded soon after, asking me to come to the planning room. I joined Freya and Ava in the room once again to discuss Samuel.

Freya sat across from us. "He decided to return in the morning this time, likely assuming no one would be awake to see him. Where is he going that takes him an entire day?"

"Perhaps," Ava started to say, "he is performing covert actions in enemy territory."

"If he were doing so, why wouldn't he tell us? Why would he cast this much suspicion on himself?" I posited.

"Maybe he was concerned we would attempt to prevent him because of the danger," Ava replied.

Freya straightened the map on the table, "If we were to assume he is, in fact, performing covert actions in Krisprelli's territory, it is still rather concerning he would not tell us. Even if he isn't planning against us, the fact that he would not tell us should still cause us concern, should it not? Someone who would not tell us of their actions is someone who could be yet more untrustworthy in the future."

"Are you saying that if we were to prove his innocence, you still would not trust Samuel?" Ava spoke with a touch of hostility in her words.

"That is exactly what I'm saying. It would be a relief to prove Samuel innocent, but I would still be concerned by the secrecy he's enshrouded his recent actions in."

"I agree with Freya here," I spoke up after some time. "Even if we could prove Samuel has done nothing wrong, because he has tried to hide his actions does bring me some concern."

"I . . . I suppose I would have to agree with you on that point," Ava conceded. "His secrecy has been rather concerning. What shall we do if we can confirm he has been preparing something against us?"

Freya stood up. "It will depend on the severity of what he is plotting. At the minimum, we'll imprison him. At the worst, well, we will have to see."

Ava started to leave the room. "Let us hope it will be nothing, then."

"You can go if you want to, Nate. There's little else I have to say."

I didn't want to leave her. "How are we holding out in Lunarford? In Wealdsey as a whole?"

She sighed. "Krisprelli's sent a few more squads to attempt to drive us from the city, but the troops have been able to fight off all of them. Our hold over the city is firm, but as long as Krisprelli is sending forces, we can't say we have full control of the city."

"And has Fredric sent us any more letters about Krisprelli's plans?"

"Not recently, no. We're currently blind to his plans. We'll keep fighting until we can say for sure the city belongs to the Opposition, hopefully with the state following soon after."

"And Aleksei," I asked, "have we been able to bring him to safety?"

"Not yet, but he's been keeping up communications with us, so we know he's currently safe. We'll send forces to find him once it's secure enough for us to do so."

"Understood. I'll let you continue with your plans for now, then."

Freya was inspecting her maps as I left the room, continuing to plot tactics. How much longer would we continue to fight this war? We had grown tired and fatigued yet continued to fight since it was the only option we had. And what were we to do if we won this war? Recovering from the losses would likely take years, and we would have to reestablish democracy in the nation. Was I to take power until we could hold proper elections, or would we begin elections immediately after Krisprelli's rule was abolished from the nation?

I could hear Samuel working in his office as I walked by the door. In a way, it caused me more unease to have him in the base than to have him absent. Perhaps it was because he could enact plots against us while he was here. We needed ways to gather evidence, but there was no way we could do so without Samuel discovering what we were doing. Would we only get evidence if he acted on his plans?

To pass the time, I decided to go to the surveillance room to watch the drone feeds. It helped occupy my mind and calm the thoughts of Samuel. The feed was largely uneventful as our troops marched around Lunarford with no Royal Army forces coming to oppose them. After a little while, Ava walked into the room.

She sat down in the chair next to mine. "The governors want to hold a meeting."

"What is the meeting for?"

"They didn't say. I just got a message from Lawrence saying we need to hold another meeting today. They should be calling soon."

Freya joined us in the surveillance room, but as expected, Samuel did not. We waited for some time, watching the video from the drones. Around half an hour passed with nothing eventful happening on the video feeds, and finally, the governors began the call. Lawrence, Margaret, Marie, and Cassius were on the screen, but Sylvestor was not in attendance.

"Where is Sylvestor?" I asked before anyone else had a chance to say anything.

"He did not want to attend the meeting today," Cassius replied. "He's still upset by the exchange with Freya the other day."

"What I said to him was deserved! He had no reason to question my plans."

"Yes, I would agree with you, but the fact stands that Sylvestor was still angered by it."

"May we move on to what we called this meeting for?" Marie asked.

"Yes," Lawrence said. "We should, although I do have to ask where Samuel is, Nate."

"He's locked himself inside his office," I answered. "He's become increasingly unpredictable and secretive. We're rather concerned about his actions. He disappeared twice within the last few days and returned very late at night or very early in the morning."

"And do you have any idea where he went during that time?"

"Not a clue. We've been watching him whenever possible, but it's impossible to do so when he locks his door. We have no clues—no evidence to prove any wrongdoing or any to prove his innocence."

Margaret spoke up. "Nate, what exactly is it you are concerned about in regard to Samuel?"

"The secrecy of his actions and his long absences are the main causes for our concern. We do not know if he could be planning something or what it could be."

"And what do you intend to do if you can prove his guilt?"

"We will decide that by the degree of his plans," Freya spoke up. "Hopefully, we will only need to imprison him, if we need to do anything."

Lawrence was looking over some papers and then spoke again. "Let us hope he isn't planning anything, then."

We discussed our upcoming plans and asked about Aleksei, timeframes, and resources, until finally Lawrence called the meeting to an end. "We have some business to attend to here, so we'll be ending the meeting," he said.

The screens clicked off and then switched back on to the video feed from the drones. The feeds were as uneventful as before; our soldiers held the city with no RA coming to oppose them. We all stayed in the room for some time, watching the screens and making small talk. Ava decided to stay and watch the feeds, while Freya and I left the room to perform our own activities. Freya returned to her planning room, and I walked about the base. I could still hear Samuel in his office as I walked by it.

How could we possibly gain any evidence to prove Samuel's guilt or his innocence? And how could we gain any clues about where he had gone? He would notice if we picked the locks to his office and searched inside, and he would likely put his plan into action sooner than planned. Was our paranoia and distrust of Samuel unfounded and unreasonable? How long could it be until we would know?

I had grown to consider Samuel a friend, someone I could trust. If we did find he was plotting against us, I would have to consider how trustworthy everyone else was. How far would Samuel's plan go, if he did have a plan to begin with? If we proved Samuel was guilty, would I despise him immediately afterward? Perhaps it would come to depend on the severity of his plans the same way it would decide the repercussions he would face for what he did.

Then an Opposition member approached me. "Nate, may I speak with you for a moment?"

"Of course! What do you need to talk with me about?"

"It's about Samuel. Perhaps you've already been told, but it's valuable information."

"Well, what is it?" I asked eagerly.

"When he came back this morning, he came through the entrance to the barracks carrying a briefcase in one hand and clutching what seemed to be a book in the other. He did not notice anyone watching him, likely because he rushed inside and was running."

I remembered the scene and said, "I was awakened by his running. I saw him go into his office. He locked the door right after he entered, which was quite audible because of the speed at which he locked it."

"What do you suspect he might be doing?"

"We believe he could be plotting against us, but without any concrete evidence, we can't say for sure. It would be rather difficult for us to get evidence unless he were to carelessly leave it out in the open, and I highly doubt he would do such a thing."

"And what if he were to execute his plan before we have the evidence to stop him?"

"Let us try not to worry about such a thing unless it occurs."

"Of course. I'll let you be on your way, then." The Opposition member, whose name I did not think to ask, walked away, and I continued on my way. I decided to go back to the surveillance room where Ava had been watching the cameras for some time now. She seemed uninterested watching them, but she would not say so directly. I sat down in the chair next to her and watched the screens.

"Anything happening?" I asked.

"Nothing of interest. Krisprelli hasn't sent any more of his soldiers to the city since yesterday. Freya said he could be waiting to send a mass assault force in an attempt to overwhelm us."

"We'll fight off everyone he can send at us until this war is over. In time, the Opposition will retake Walneyria."

"Our soldiers will need supplies soon—food, ammo, more medicine. Their basic needs."

"I'll get supplies ready and pack them into a truck to take them to Lunarford. I'll travel with a few of our soldiers for defense."

"Thank you, Nate. Travel carefully."

I went to the barracks and assembled a crate of supplies the soldiers in Lunarford would need. A few of the troops still at the base helped me assemble the supplies, and we had everything prepared after about an hour. We carried the box to a truck and loaded it carefully. After putting on our armor and picking up our weapons in case we were ambushed by Royal Army patrols, we all got into the truck.

The ride was, again, unremarkable, and we were able to drive straight to Lunarford rather than march to the city as we had before. We distributed the supplies to the soldiers in Lunarford and stayed behind for some time to talk with them and encourage them. Everyone we talked to said it was a simple defense, as the Royal Army had not tried to retake the city since the previous day.

Suddenly, Freya's voice came through my helmet. "You're going to be stuck in Lunarford for some time. My assumption was right. Krisprelli's sending a massive group of his troops toward the area. Order the snipers to high ground, and prepare for a difficult fight."

I remained calm and did as Freya said. The snipers got to high ground as quickly as they could, while the ground troops got behind cover. Those with gravity fields powered them on. Over the horizon, we saw dozens, well over a hundred, Royal Army soldiers marching toward us. The snipers took out the ones equipped with heavier armor, while those of us on the ground fired into the crowd of soldiers. The standoff for Lunarford had begun.

CHAPTER THIRTEEN

Krisprelli's forces were numerous and had us pinned on all sides. We fought them off for endless hours, but they continued to advance. Some of their snipers were able to kill a few of our soldiers before our snipers took them out. Others lobbed grenades, which heavily injured several troops and killed others. At last, we had a slight respite when the encroaching soldiers let up. I helped with the injured, administering Sanitatem Celer to treat their wounds until Ava could treat them properly. Others picked up the dead and laid them with care next to one another until we could give them proper burials.

"I doubt those bodies will be the last we face today," a soldier said to me.

"There's more approaching," Freya said through the comms. "I'd say you have about 15 minutes, give or take, until they get there."

"Understood. Is Samuel still in his office?"

"One of the people we had watching the doors told us when he left. We tried to follow him with a drone, but it seems he saw it and took it down."

"Took it down? How?"

"It looked like he threw something at it. It wouldn't take much to knock one of them down. We saw it falling, but its video cut out when it impacted the ground."

"What direction was he traveling?"

"It looked like he was going toward Goldheart, but we have no way to know where he went after he took out the drone."

"And his office?"

"Locked, of course. He doesn't want us to find out anything."

"We'll find something out soon enough. We can't allow him to trap us in his plots."

"Definitely. Now, get back to fighting. They'll be there soon."

I continued treating the wounded for a few more minutes and then got back into position. As the Royal Army began marching into view, they had the appearance of a horde. Our snipers carefully watched for Royal Army snipers and took them out as they made their way to high ground. Once more, we began firing into the horde of soldiers. Before we could stop them, an enemy soldier hurled a grenade into the middle of a large group of our soldiers, but one of them jumped on top of the grenade to protect the others. That soldier died, but she saved all the other lives around her.

We continued fighting for several more hours, far into the dark of night. The Royal Army soldiers had hardly shrunk in number as we fought; each one we took down seemed to be instantly replaced by another. Our troops had to rush to help those injured before they bled out from the wounds. Many injuries were due to explosives, while others were due to concentrated fire in the same spot on the armor. Once we had put down every RA troop we could see, we finally rested.

We separated the troops into groups of 20. Three groups would rest for two hours, while the other groups would stand guard to watch for the Royal Army. I specifically assigned myself to one of the groups who would have the longest wait until they rested since I did not want to seem weak to the others. The next several hours passed with no more troops marching toward Lunarford, which allowed our soldiers to get some much-needed rest. Once the first groups had rested, they took the dead and injured back to Esterden and returned to Lunarford not long afterward.

"Samuel's back." Ava's voice played through my helmet. "He didn't rush in like yesterday, but he locked himself in his office all the same."

"Damn it! And we still have no idea where he went and what he's doing. Was he carrying anything with him this time?"

"The book and briefcase he was carrying when he came back yesterday. He was holding the book as if to hide its cover from any onlookers. Perhaps the cover of that book would give us a clue to what he's doing."

"A clue or maybe the answer entirely," I said. "Perhaps that book is the one I saw him writing in the other day. I didn't get a glimpse of its cover, though."

"He was writing in it? If that is, in fact, the same book, then it's a notebook. If we could get our hands on it, it would no doubt have clues—evidence for or against Samuel. We need to get our hands on that book if at all possible." Her voice was urgent.

"Definitely. If that book would proffer us the evidence we're in search of, getting our hands on it without Samuel knowing would be incredibly important."

"We could attempt to catch him the next time he leaves his office and keep him in our prison."

"No, that's too risky," I said. "If he's acting against us, he could kill anyone who attempted to detain him."

"And you think it's safer to allow him to repeatedly leave the base while we have no knowledge of where he's going?"

"It is more immediately safe, but in the long run, we do need to stop him once we have found suitable evidence against him."

"Nate,"—Freya joined in on the conversation—"Ava has a point. If we keep allowing Samuel to leave our sight when we don't have even the smallest inkling of where he's going, it's incredibly unsafe. We need to do something before he brings us harm."

"We'll consider plans once I've returned to Esterden. I'll remain in Lunarford for the time being."

I cut off the long-range comms for the helmet, leaving only those near me in Lunarford to communicate with me. We would need to keep watching Samuel incredibly carefully to stop him from setting off any traps he had potentially set. It was almost guaranteed at this point that he was plotting something, but what was it? Was it to help us or to bring harm on us? Hopefully, the answers I sought would come soon enough.

We continued our shifts in Lunarford for several more hours, patrolling whenever we weren't resting. The city had not been ravaged too badly by the fighting, at least not outside the main city center where the combat had largely been focused. Random gunshots and damage from explosions marked a few of the buildings we came across. Hopefully, we would not have to wait long until Krisprelli left the city.

Once daylight came, the Royal Army again started marching toward the city. The groups were smaller than before, however; and we had an easier time fighting them this time. They also were not able to inflict as many casualties on us as they had the previous day. Once we finished fighting, I turned the long-range communications back on inside my helmet.

Freya started speaking soon after. "The fact he's sending smaller numbers of troops toward the city is a good sign. He'll likely keep sending people, but we'll have better odds in the fight now."

"Indeed. Hopefully, we'll capture the city soon enough," I said. "And where is Samuel?"

"He's still in his office."

"Good."

Freya did not say anything more for some time, so neither did I. Then I helped the few soldiers who had been injured in the fight, but fortunately, we did not lose anyone this time. We were clear for a couple of hours until another large group came over the hills.

We fought them off just as we had before, the snipers picking some off and the rest of the soldiers taking out the bulk of the forces. It had become like a dreadful routine at that point. Once we had taken out every RA troop threatening our hold on the city, we returned to our shifts, resting and patrolling. I helped treat the injured and then patrolled for some time.

Once again, we brought the injured back to Esterden, and this time, I went with those who were taking them. We carried the wounded into the medical ward, and the uninjured soldiers who had medical knowledge aided them until Ava was able to. After around an hour, the uninjured returned to Lunarford, but I stayed in Esterden. I went to the surveillance room where Ava and Freya still were and locked the door behind me, just in case Samuel tried to enter.

"Ah, Nate," Ava said as I entered. "Good to see you. We can discuss what to do about Samuel now that you're back."

"I still say that detaining him is a good idea," Freya said without looking up from the screen.

"It's not worth the risk," I said. "He could murder anyone who tried to do so." I couldn't believe we were talking about Samuel, a man we'd considered a friend but was now a potential murderer, a traitor.

"And you think keeping him free and allowing him to wander off and do whatever he wishes is safer?" Ava shouted.

"I do not believe it to be safer entirely, but it would be immediately safer until we have devised a plan to deal with Samuel properly."

"Nate," Freya spoke once more, "we need to come up with a plan soon. We don't know how close Samuel might be to completing his plans. If we don't stop him soon, we may not have a chance at all."

"Bar his office from the outside, then. That will keep him locked up."

Ava crossed her arms. "He would starve, we wouldn't be able to watch him, and we wouldn't get any evidence. That would be an utterly useless plan."

"Then what do you suggest we do?" I was getting frustrated.

"If detaining him would present too much of a risk, then we will just need to keep watching him. We can lock the doors to the base at any time to try to keep Samuel locked inside. We could mask it as a safety measure."

"In a way," Freya said with a smirk, "it is a safety measure. We'd be preventing Samuel from leaving, thus preventing him from furthering the progress of his plans."

"And how could we prevent him from leaving when we unlock the doors for entering and exiting the building?" I asked.

Ava thought for a moment. "We only unlock the doors we are using to enter and exit the building and carefully watch for Samuel. If he tries to leave, we stop him and give him the excuse that we need him at the base for a meeting."

"And what if we don't have a meeting for that day?"

"We'll call the governors and get them to host a fake meeting for us to keep up the lie. As long as we can prevent him from leaving the base, we'll be safe."

Freya stood up from her seat. "We would need to speak with the governors early in the day to tell them we need to call them up for a fake meeting. As long as they know beforehand, they'll help us."

Freya left the room, and Ava left soon after. I watched the screens for a few minutes more before I left the room. Everything felt more hectic in the last several days. Nothing can ever feel calm during a time like this, but everything that had happened recently felt more intense than the days before. We needed to find the evidence necessary to have an answer as to Samuel's alignment. How long might it be until we had that evidence?

I went to my room and lay down in bed, sleeping restlessly just as I had several nights in a row. My thoughts once again kept me awake as I remembered those who had been injured in Lunarford and those who had died, especially the soldier who had jumped on the grenade to save those around her. Would she be remembered, or would her name simply be listed among all the other names of the war dead with few people remembering who she was and what she had done in her life? As I fell asleep, I promised myself that for as long as I lived, I would not forget her or her sacrifice.

CHAPTER FOURTEEN

I paid little attention to the thoughts going through my mind as I rose from my bed. There was a small file on my desk, the Opposition's sigil stamped on it. I picked it up and opened it quickly, hoping it contained clues about Samuel. But all that was in it were transcripts of various conversations Samuel had with other Opposition members, adding little more than a list of more people who shared in the paranoia that had spread throughout the base.

I wanted to take note of anything Samuel said in the transcripts that was of particular interest, but nothing gave me any major clues. Samuel had a skill of using words to his advantage and using them against others, which allowed him to gain the position he had in the Opposition. Had he used his words against us as well? I set the folder back down on my desk after I read every word in its contents.

For some time, I stared blankly at the wall, drifting into a daydream or maybe simply a state of deep concentration. Several questions began to swirl through my mind like a tempest. How many of us would be left when this war was done? Would we turn out as the victors, or would Krisprelli eventually crush us underneath his heel? And most importantly, where did Samuel's allegiance lie?

Ava came into my room and jarred me out of the trance I had entered. She said nothing as she pulled me into her workshop, once again to show me another one of her constructions. Freya was also in the room, sitting down but not wearing the robotic legs that I had not seen her without since the first time she put them on. Ava was working on something at one of the tables, obfuscating my view of it.

I sat down next to Freya. "Do you not need the legs anymore?"

"I don't absolutely need to have them as I did when Ava first gave them to me, but it's still much easier for me to walk with them for now while I finish my recovery. She's been working on refining the legs, making the movements more fluid, things like that. Due to our limited resources for such a project, Ava's working on them by simply upgrading the original pair she first constructed."

"I'm simply changing out the motors and rewiring the neural link functions; it's nothing overly complicated," Ava said while still working on the legs.

Freya had a light smile on her face. "I swear she sometimes doesn't realize how smart she is."

"It definitely seems that way at times, doesn't it?"

"Do you think she realizes the brilliance of the things she's created in this workshop alone, Nate? The impact of everything she's made here is incredible. The armor plating, the gravity technology, the legs she's built, the medicine. When she has access to a proper workshop again with good supplies, she'll change the face of our world even more."

"You make it sound as if I'm some amazingly wonderous inventor, Freya."

"And? Are you not a wonderful inventor?"

"I suppose it would depend on who you ask."

"Well, then, Nate, what do you think?"

"You're a brilliantly talented, incredibly intelligent inventor, Ava."

"That settles it, then!" Freya said happily, playfully hitting me on my shoulder.

I missed times like this—times when we could all come together and not have to worry about anything incredibly important in our lives, times when we could enjoy a sense of friendship and camaraderie. I hadn't shared any moments like that with Freya before the war began, but I would fight even harder to share times like this after the war.

"The motors are working as expected," Ava said, still crouched over her worktable. "I'll just need a few more minutes to finish the reworks on the neural link pathways, and then the legs will be ready to go."

"Nate,"—Freya spoke quietly now—"let's try to make the rest of the day as enjoyable as these past few hours have been. We need a day in which we have few things to cause us stress."

"But what of Samuel? Our fighting in Lunarford? That file that was left in my room?"

"I left that file in there in case you were still curious. We'll talk about all of that later, but for now, we need time to relax."

"They're done," Ava exclaimed excitedly. "Every change that was needed is done; the legs are ready for you once more, Freya."

Freya stood up from her chair and walked over to the legs. She was able to put them on by herself this time, showing how well she had recovered from her injury. Walking around the room, her gait seemed natural and no different than how she had walked before. In other words, the legs still worked, but with more fluidity and precision.

Freya hugged Ava tightly. "Thank you for everything you've done for us. And everything you'll do for the world when we're done."

Ava began tearing up at Freya's words and returned the hug. Freya was a compassionate woman, though she seldom showed it outwardly. She had a deep respect for Ava, as we all did. Ava knew that, but she was still incredibly touched by Freya's words. Ava would bring great changes to the world once she did not have to dedicate her time to supporting the Opposition and treating injured soldiers.

"How should we spend the rest of our day? It's much too early to let this feeling of calm leave us," Ava said as she sat down.

"We could tell stories," I replied, "or play a few of the games I have in my room."

"Spending a few hours playing games sounds like a wonderful idea."

I went back to my room and grabbed a few of the games I had saved. I carefully listened to Samuel's office as I passed by, making sure he was still inside. Even while I enjoyed a calm day with Freya and Ava, my anxiety did not abate from being concerned about Samuel. I pushed the feeling aside and went back to the workshop where Ava had moved a table for us to play games.

We spent the next several hours playing board games and telling stories. It was a good day. Once we had played every game a few times, we decided to just tell stories for a little while longer. It was wonderful to be able to spend time like that—even if only for a day—not worried about war and death. The day had become late by the time we all had run out of stories to tell, so Freya decided to turn to the more serious matters at hand.

"We need to decide what to do about Samuel. We still haven't come up with a plan."

Ava was quiet for a moment. "Hadn't we decided we would keep the exit doors locked when we did not need them to prevent Samuel from leaving?"

"Yes, we did, but we haven't made any plan for what we'll do to get clues. We're still completely blind to his plans."

"We need to somehow drive him out of his office," I said, "and then get inside and look for anything important."

"Too risky," Freya said. "He'll only leave his office for something incredibly important, and he'd notice if we had gone inside and moved anything."

Ava tapped her chin. "What if we put small cameras and microphones in the room to watch him?"

"That could work," Freya began, "but they'd have to be small enough that Samuel wouldn't discover them."

"Freya," I spoke up, "about that folder you left in my room."

"Yes, what about it?"

"There wasn't anything of much use in it; nothing Samuel said in any of those conversations was overtly suspicious."

"That's unfortunate. I was hoping we could get something important out of them."

Ava walked over to her worktable. "I'll work on getting a few small cameras and microphones ready. You two can come up with a plan to get Samuel to leave his office."

Freya and I got up and left the workshop so Ava could work. We walked to the planning room and sat down, both of us quiet for a moment. How close were we to uncovering Samuel's plot? Would we get the answers we'd been looking for? Freya broke the silence after a few more minutes.

"He wouldn't leave his office for something that wasn't an emergency."

"Definitely not," I replied.

"Perhaps we lock his office doors once he's left them but with a magnetic lock so he can't open it with his key. We get someone to occupy him. Then Ava sneaks inside and puts in the cameras and mics. We unlock the door, Ava gets out, and Samuel never knows."

"Wouldn't Ava need the key to his office to get inside?"

"A magnetic lock unlocks a key lock when turned on. We turn it on to unlock the door, turn it off for Ava to get inside, lock it again until she's done putting in the cameras and mics, and then unlock it for her to get out."

"That seems like a rather intricate plan," I said. "What if Samuel tries to come back too early, or what if he sees Ava go inside?"

"We let him get near one of the exit doors; that's when we'll get someone to distract him. His office doors won't be in his view."

"I suppose it's as good a plan as any, then. We just need to wait for Ava to have the cameras ready."

Freya called Ava with the communication hub. "When do you think the cameras will be done?"

"It'll be tomorrow at the earliest," Ava replied. "Lots of little pieces I need to fit in just right. Hard to do with what I have here."

"Okay, thank you," Freya said as she ended the call.

I leaned back in my chair. "Tomorrow at the earliest, then."

"Indeed."

"What should we do until then?"

"We wait for what we need to be ready, and then we wait for the opening to set our plan in motion."

"I'll go back to my room for now. I'll talk with you later, Freya."

Freya smiled at me as I walked out the door, not saying anything. Samuel was still inside his office, and I could hear him as I walked by. Soon, we would know about what he'd been planning. I went in my room and lay on the bed, letting the happier thoughts of the day overcome the unhappy thoughts about Samuel. My dreams that night were quite pleasant for the first night in some time.

I woke up the next morning feeling calm and unworried. There was a letter on the floor inside my door. It was addressed to me from Fredric Solsthar. Why had he addressed the letter to me directly? I tucked the letter into my jacket and went to Ava's workshop, seeing that Freya was already inside. Ava was still working on the cameras as I entered.

"Morning, Nate," Freya said to me as I sat down.

"Hey, Freya. How long have you been awake?"

"An hour, maybe. You?"

"Just a few minutes. There was something interesting in my room when I woke up, though. A letter from Fredric."

"A letter from Fredric? What did it say?"

"I haven't opened it yet. I figured I should wait until we could all hear it."

"Read it," Ava said, still working. "Nothing much better to do right now anyway."

I opened the envelope and took out the letter. "'Krisprelli's become more upset with the advances the Opposition made into his territory,'" I read, "'and he's launching a two-pronged assault. He'll be sending forces toward your base while still attempting to retake Lunarford.'"

Ava stepped away from her worktable, "My god! Tell Samuel. He needs to know, too."

"He could be the very person behind this!" I said.

"Tell everyone," Freya said. "No one can afford to be in the dark about this."

I went to the surveillance room where the intercom system was. The system could broadcast throughout the entire base, and I remained calm as I read the letter for everyone to hear. I did not want to worry anyone more than they already would be. Deep down, I was terrified by what was going to happen to us, but outwardly, I did not let it show. Were we about to be killed?

CHAPTER FIFTEEN

I walked out of the surveillance room to go back to the workshop. Once I was downstairs, I saw Ava and Freya walking toward the planning room, so we headed in together and sat down at the table. Ava was carrying a tray with the cameras and microphones she had been working on, while Freya pulled out a map of Esterden. We were all still paranoid, but for a different reason than we had been.

"The base doesn't have any sort of defensive mechanisms built into it, so we'll need to rely on the soldiers we have at the base for defense," Freya said as she looked over the map.

I studied the map. "And we won't be able to call anyone back from Lunarford; they need to be there for defense."

"We have 50 healthy soldiers still here, give or take a few. We'll get them ready, and they'll march outside to defend against the Royal Army when they approach. Our snipers will go up on the roof. It's not very high ground, but it's better than nothing."

"If we are still worried about Samuel," Ava said as she set down the tray, "I've finished working on the cameras."

Freya pushed the map aside as she sat back down. "If the opportunity to put the cameras in his office presents itself without the use of the plan we came up with, you should put them there. Otherwise, we'll be unconcerned with Samuel's actions once we're dealing with the more pressing issues facing us."

"What will we do if Krisprelli's troops reach the base?" I asked.

"We'll be imprisoned or killed," Ava replied. "The Royal Army will march through the Opposition States unopposed, save for Lunarford, and the war will have been for nothing."

"While grim, she's right," Freya said as she stood up. "If we're overrun today, it'll be the end of the Opposition. We need to fight as hard as we can."

I thought for a moment about those words. It was true that if our base was taken by Krisprelli's forces, it would end the war, but I was shocked by how easily Freya and Ava had been able to say it. Maybe they weren't as scared of death as I was, or maybe they accepted death more easily than I did. I had to steady myself for a moment before I spoke again. "We should get the troops ready. We can't be unprepared for when the Royal Army approaches."

"Yes, let's go," Freya replied as she walked out the door.

Ava and I walked with Freya to the barracks. As we headed in, we saw everyone already in their armor and carrying their other equipment, prepared for battle. They waved at us as we entered and then carried on getting everything in order and making sure everyone had their things. Freya went around checking whether anyone was missing any piece of their equipment and then rejoined Ava and me at the front of the room. Ava called for everyone's attention and began to speak.

"Your fight here today may come to be one of the most decisive battles of this war. If we lose here today, we've lost entirely. Fight harder than you've fought before, win this battle, and protect us from the Royal Army so we may all live to fight another day."

The soldiers clapped for the speech and finished their preparations. We unlocked the exit door in the barracks, and the soldiers filed outside and began their marches around the base. Before we left the barracks, I decided to put on my armor and take a pistol, just in case. We began to leave the barracks and walk to the surveillance room to watch the cameras in Lunarford. As we were walking up the stairs,

Samuel came up to us. We all acted calm as he began to speak so as not to arouse his suspicion.

"It's been some time since we all spoke, hasn't it?" Samuel said as he stepped next to us.

I hesitated for a moment. "Y-yeah, it has."

"Something wrong, Nate? You seem worried." He didn't look me in the eye.

"Just worried about today, our safety. That's all." I told a half lie.

Why was Samuel suddenly trying to talk to us after several days of locking himself away? More importantly, why had he been acting as if it were nothing? He was doing nothing to make himself less suspicious, but I, of course, could not say that right now. What was he trying to do? I stopped thinking about it for now and focused on the conversation.

"Come on," Freya said, "to the surveillance room."

We walked to the surveillance room and sat down in front of the screens. Ava flew the drones to different points above Lunarford so their views could cover the widest area. For now, the city was uncontested, and our forces held it firmly, but that would change. Several minutes passed before we saw Royal Army forces marching toward the city. The group was not very numerous, and our forces fired at them once they were in range.

The fighting went just as it had when I was in Lunarford. Shots were exchanged, Royal Army soldiers were killed, and our people were injured by explosions. Some of the explosions killed a few of our soldiers. The other soldiers helped the injured when they could rush to cover from the gunfire. After some time, our troops completely took out the first group of Royal Army forces.

The lull in battle did not last long, however; and more Royal Army troops came over the hills. A grenade thrown by a Royal Army soldier killed several of our soldiers who had not seen it in time, and the fighting continued in the same manner for several more hours.

"They're fighting hard to take back Lunarford," Ava said. "They'll likely fight even harder against us here at the base."

Ava flew a few drones over the base and switched some of the screens to their feeds. For now, they showed our soldiers marching around the perimeter of the building and our snipers on the roof. For now, the base was secure. How much longer would we have before our safety here was threatened?

We watched the camera feeds from both locations at the same time, the cameras for the base showing little of interest, while the cameras in Lunarford continued to show combat. Several more of our people were injured, with a few more joining the dead. Several more hours passed until the fighting subsided for longer than just a few minutes. It seemed as if the Royal Army had begun to leave Lunarford.

"If they're leaving Lunarford, that means they'll be coming toward us now," Freya said, sounding afraid.

She notified the soldiers, telling them to stay extra vigilant. There was a tense feeling in the room, a feeling of an impending dread. Ava was watching the screens, not saying anything, likely to hide the fear she was feeling. Freya continued talking with the soldiers, making sure they stayed watchful, and instructed them not to hold their fire for any circumstance. She stayed strong under the intense pressure we were facing.

Samuel had not said anything during the battle, which had been unnerving in its own way. His mere presence was eerie, and the silence he had developed only added to that. While he had never been one to say much, he also hadn't ever been this quiet for so long. I was worried, but I tried to think little of it. I kept watching the screens, looking for Royal Army forces.

"Let's take some time to calm down," Ava said, "before the worst of it begins."

We spent a few minutes telling some jokes and singing a few songs to lighten the mood and bring some calm, if only for a few moments. Samuel even joined in with us, which surprised me. It alleviated the concern I felt by his presence but did not nullify it entirely. We turned our attention back to the drone feeds and kept watching for Krisprelli's forces to approach the base.

Freya spoke suddenly: "This could be the last day we're all alive. That just hit me. Damn! That scares me."

"We'll live," I replied. "We have to. If we die here today, we'll have died for little reason. That doesn't suit us even slightly."

"Death is not determined by how fitting it is for the victim to die when they do. It takes you whenever it decides to. I would think you of all people would agree with me on that, Nate."

"I suppose you're correct. But I'm sure we'll live past today."

Freya said nothing more and turned back to the screen. The proximity of death had definitely occurred to me, yet it did not scare me. Right now, I felt at peace with death. I kept watching the screen, thinking about the peace I had in that moment.

That was until a gunshot rang out. It wasn't through the audio from the drone. It came from inside the surveillance room.

Samuel had shot Ava in the arm, and Freya jumped up to stop the bleeding. I lunged onto Samuel, wrestling him to the ground as he let loose another shot, which hit my armor. Forcing the gun from his hand, I hurled it across the room and then stabbed him in the chest with my gauntlet blade. I managed to avoid any immediately lethal spot in order to allow him to speak to us. I left the blade in his chest as I slowly stood up so as not to hurry the flow of blood.

"I knew we were right to suspect you, you bastard! What have you been plotting? Is anyone working with you?" I screamed.

Samuel's speech was uneven. "I-I'm sorry, truly . . . I did not want to hurt anyone, but I had to."

"What reason would you ever have to harm any of us?"

"To protect—protect my son. Krisprelli has him. He gave me a choice."

"Your son? A choice? What choice?"

"Th-the police, the ones who were looking for rebels back when Krisprelli first took power, back when the Opposition was still new, found out that I—that I was working with you. Krisprelli didn't know who else was a part of the group, so he gave me the choice of working as a double agent. He . . . he took my son as "collateral," told me he'd kill him if I didn't work against you. I'm so sorry."

"Your secrecy, your random disappearances, when you started acting more irritable and unpredictable—that was all because you were working as a double agent? How far back do your plans go, Samuel?"

"S-several months, before the war even began. When we were attacked in Highborough."

"You were the one who told them where we were?"

"The war was inevitable. I incited it sooner than it would have begun otherwise. Once the war began, more options presented themselves to me to begin further plans. When the Opposition took Goldheart, Krisprelli threatened me. I needed to work faster to stop the Opposition or else he'd . . . he would kill my son. That's when I started leaving the base. I was going to Krisprelli's hold and bargaining with him to give me more time. Once the movements in Wealdsey began, once we took Lunarford . . . "

"We?"

"Th-the Opposition. I still consider myself a member, even though I have been working against the efforts, but my hand was forced."

"What happened when we took Lunarford?"

"I . . . I had to keep negotiating with Krisprelli for him to give me more time before he killed my son. I presented a plan to him, and he gave me as much time as I needed to execute it."

"And what was that plan?"

"I told him Fredric was a spy, and he forced him to write the letter you read. I was the one who slipped it under your door. The plan was to cause paranoia at the base and have as few soldiers around as possible. He'd keep sending forces to Lunarford, but the part of the letter that said they were going to attack the base was false. If the plan had succeeded, I . . . I would have gathered all three of you in this room, as I did, but I would have killed all of you. Once you were dead, he would actually send forces to attack the base, kill the small number of soldiers still here, then take out the rest of the forces in Lunarford to end the war."

"Jesus . . . that's a detailed plan. Was Fredric killed after you revealed him as a spy?"

"K-Krisprelli had him killed, yes. I-I'm sorry for everything I've done, Nate. I know you can't forgive me. I don't want you to forgive me. I . . . "

"I can understand why you did it. You had the chance to get back the loved one who was taken from you. You did everything you could to get him back. I can't forgive you, but I understand."

"Thank you, Nate. Goodbye."

Samuel took his last breath as he bled out on the floor, and I pulled my blade from his body. It hurt to feel so betrayed by someone I had considered a friend, even if we were suspecting him of something. He had an understandable reason, but it was still painful to be betrayed, and it somehow hurt even more to be the one to take his life. He was another casualty of Krisprelli's regime, and double agent or not, he was our friend. I felt he still cared for us in the end, and his reason for acting against us was his son's life, which Krisprelli held over his head. Because Samuel could no longer report to him, Krisprelli would kill his son without a second thought. We would make Krisprelli pay for this once we got to him.

CHAPTER SIXTEEN

I pulled off my armor and then rushed to the medical ward to get a bottle of Sanitatem Celer for Ava's wound. One of the Opposition members who had medical knowledge came to the surveillance room to quickly remove the bullet from Ava's arm. She cleaned the wound, dripped some of the Sanitatem onto it, and then checked for any other injuries. Once she was sure Ava had no further injuries, she left the room, saying nothing about Samuel's body.

Freya spoke into the comms system to tell the soldiers the Royal Army wouldn't be coming to the base and to come back inside. They returned to the barracks to rest. We had not yet told them about Samuel. Freya and I cleaned the blood around Samuel's body and then took it to the morgue until we could bury him with the full attendance of every member of the Opposition.

Samuel had gone against us and engaged in long-term conspiracy, but his hand had been forced. Krisprelli was a twisted individual and did whatever he pleased to keep his power over the country, but at times it felt as if he chose to do specifically the most painful things to those he affected. In the case of Samuel, Krisprelli's cruelty had been to force Samuel to plot against us to keep his son alive.

"We need to tell everyone," Ava said, "everyone here on base, the soldiers in Lunarford, and the governors."

"Definitely," I replied. "We'll tell our people in detail later, and we'll tell the governors when we call them."

I broadcast across the base again, saying that Samuel was dead and nothing more. Freya told the soldiers in Lunarford. We sent a message to Lawrence telling him we needed to hold a meeting, and he replied that he would be able to the next morning. Freya, Ava, and I went back to each of our rooms to rest. I had to let it sink in that Samuel was really, truly dead.

Samuel, a person I had thought of as a friend for so long now, someone I truly trusted, was dead. He had gone against us, he was going to try to kill me, and by all means I had every right in the world to hate him. And yet I didn't, because his actions, though they were against us, weren't what he would have done on his own. He was caught in a corner by a devious man and was forced to harm us to protect his son who had been taken from him. If we all had the chance to get back the people who were taken from us, we would probably do anything. And for Samuel, that meant betraying the Opposition.

How should we feel about Samuel now? Were we meant to despise him and be glad he was dead? Were we meant to cry and be sad about it? What would Krisprelli want us to feel? Whatever that was, I wanted to do the exact opposite. I was sad that Samuel was dead. As I told Samuel, I couldn't forgive him—at least not yet—but I could understand why he did what he did.

I fell asleep as I thought about what we would do to honor Samuel and if we would honor him at all. I would need to talk to Ava and Freya about what they wanted to do. Waking early the next morning, I went back up to the surveillance room for the meeting with the governors. Ava and Freya came inside a little while after I did and sat next to each other. There was an eerie feeling permeating the room that I could not shake. I realized the feeling was likely due to Samuel.

Ava broke the silence. "It'll feel rather different around here now that Samuel's gone."

"It's weird," Freya said, "but I feel . . . sad about it. Sadder than I would have expected to feel for someone who betrayed us."

I straightened up in my chair. "I feel as though it helps that Samuel didn't go against us willfully. Krisprelli forced his hand and made him participate in a demented sort of game in which he had to work against us or see his son killed. We may not forgive him, but we can agree that his actions were, arguably, understandable."

"I suppose I can agree with that," Freya said sincerely. I don't disdain Samuel now that we know for sure he was plotting against us. I just feel hurt by it—not by the betrayal itself but why he did it. Krisprelli needs to pay dearly for everything he's done."

We waited around for a few more minutes, not saying much more. We still considered Samuel a friend, yet I was the one to take Samuel's life. I tried to think little of it until the screens flashed on with the faces of the governors. Even Sylvestor was in attendance this time.

"Nate, Freya, Ava," Lawrence said, "good to see you all."

"Samuel's still not there?" asked Sylvestor, who had presumably been told about Samuel's absence from the last meeting.

"Actually," I said, "that's what we called this meeting for. Samuel's . . . Samuel's dead."

Margaret interjected, "Dead? How is he dead?"

"I had to kill him once he revealed himself to be a double agent."

"Just as we had suspected," Freya cut in.

"Do you know his motives," Marie asked, "his reasons for going against us?"

Ava answered, "Krisprelli had taken his son but not killed him. When Krisprelli found out Samuel was working for an opposition group, he gave him the choice of working against us as a double agent or letting his son die. He understandably chose the option to protect his son and began working against us."

"And," Lawrence spoke up once more, "how long has he been a double agent?"

"He was the one who told them about our base in Highborough, so it's been since before then," I replied.

Cassius spoke up now. "And he was working by himself? He hadn't gotten anyone else to aid him in his plans?"

"As far as we know, yes," Freya replied, "he was working by himself."

"Are we going to hold a funeral for him? Pay any sort of respects? What is it you want us to do?" Lawrence asked.

I thought over my words. "We want to hold a funeral for Samuel, yes. We still respect him and understand the reasons behind his actions, though we do not forgive him. We want to hold a funeral with the attendance of all Opposition members."

"We'll all be there," Sylvestor said. "Call us again once you know when it will be held. Thank you."

The screens clicked off as the call disconnected, and we all sat back in our seats. It seemed Sylvestor did not care much about what had happened with Freya the other day, or maybe it was because of Samuel's death. Our soldiers in Lunarford would have to return if we truly wanted a full Opposition attendance, so we would need to decide when it would be safe to call them back. Freya said if they spent another three days in the city without it being attacked again, it would be safe to call back all but a few soldiers who would stay behind and defend the city.

"We won't have a true full Opposition attendance," Freya said, "but it will be as close as we can possibly get. It's just a necessity to have soldiers remain in Lunarford so Krisprelli can't send his troops to the city while it is entirely undefended."

"Yes," I said, "I understand. I just feel sad for the troops who won't be able to return for the funeral."

"I understand. I'll see if we can set up screens or some way for them to watch it from a live feed."

"I could get it set up," Ava said. "It'd be little more than modifying a drone feed."

Ava walked out of the surveillance room to go back to her workshop and work on a way for the troops in Lunarford to see the funeral. Freya and I remained in the surveillance room since we both had little to do. The feeling in the base had been rather different, changing from intensity and paranoia to sadness, a kind of dread. Through Samuel, Krisprelli had been able to strike so close to us because he was an insane, manipulative tyrant and had exactly what he needed to get Samuel to go along with his plans.

Where would he stop, if he would stop anywhere? How many more people would have to suffer at the hands of Krisprelli? There were so many questions that wouldn't be answered for quite some time. I kept thinking about them as I stared absentmindedly at one of the screens.

"We could go into his office," Freya said after a few minutes, "and find out what was in that book and the briefcase he was carrying."

"Doesn't that seem a bit disrespectful? What would be the point of it, anyway? We know what he was doing, and we don't need evidence anymore. I killed him, for Christ's sake."

"I don't want them for evidence; I want to know what was in them. I'm just curious now."

"Another day, Freya. We can look at them another day. Maybe after he's actually been buried. Please?"

"Yes, of course. I'm sorry, Nathaniel."

"I've asked you not to call me that."

Freya walked out of the room, not saying anything more to me. I guess I had upset her, or maybe she was just giving me some time to myself. Either way, I went back to my room a few minutes later and sat at my desk. I stared at the wall for a while, not sure how to occupy my mind. I'd seen so many deaths since this war began, so many people injured and killed, but it had not numbed me like the feeling of the death of someone close to me. Samuel's death was painful. In a way, it felt strange caring so deeply, being so saddened by the death of someone who was a traitor, but I felt that pain all the same. It felt even stranger to be planning a funeral for him—one where hundreds of people would be attending to honor him—after he had tried to kill us. It felt so strange and surreal.

I wrote a letter on one of the pages in my notebook, a letter that no one else would ever know existed. A letter to Samuel. A letter telling him I was sorry for what he had been through and that, at last, I forgave his actions since he had been cornered into doing them. A letter he would never get to see, a letter that would never be sent. A letter I had to write to come to terms with his death. And even then, it still didn't feel quite real.

I finished writing the letter and carefully took the page out of the notebook. Tucking it into an envelope, I sealed it with wax and wrote "To Samuel" on the front of it. I put the letter into a small wooden box, which I put under my bed. Maybe somewhere, Samuel will get to read that letter, but it wouldn't be here. It never would be here. Slowly, I began to truly accept that fact.

CHAPTER SEVENTEEN

Our troops had already been in Lunarford for two days, uncontested, meaning they only had to have one more day without Krisprelli sending his troops before they could return to Esterden. It would be a short return, only for the funeral, before they would return to Lunarford. Once they returned to Wealdsey, they would need to find Aleksei to get him to safety. It felt like we had so many things to do before this war would end, and I kept thinking of it all as I fell asleep.

My dreams were dreadfully unpleasant, tinged with Samuel's blood. His death after I stabbed him kept playing in my mind, over and over, giving me not even a moment of peace. I woke up early, feeling panicked, and I could not return to sleep. Mortality had taken physicality inside of me in that moment, and this was its way of showing me that. I pushed away those feelings and got out of bed, trying not to think of that moment anymore. It was useless to let it worry me.

I left my room and saw several people milling about in the hall. They made small talk as I walked to the workshop, which was a good distraction from what had been worrying me. Ava was working on the camera from one of the drones, with a screen on the table beside it. I assumed she was attempting to get the camera's video to display on the screen but with little success.

"Hey, Nate," Ava said, fiddling with the camera. "How are you?"

"I could be better. What are you working on there?"

"Trying to get this drone camera to stream to this screen," she said. "I'll need to get a few set up, but once I get one, it won't be difficult to connect the others."

"And these are for the soldiers that'll be remaining in Lunarford?"

"Yes, so they can see Samuel's funeral."

The funeral would be a spectacular, if somber, affair. Hundreds of people would be in attendance, and it would likely take up the entire day. How many more of us would be buried before peace was reached? Would Ava or Freya be among the dead eventually, too? Would I join the dead before it was all done? My thoughts were turning increasingly dark, but I tried not to think about death again and went back to talking with Ava.

I sat up in my chair. "Are you worried, Ava?"

"About what?

"Dying. Losing this war. The Opposition's work being for nothing."

"Sometimes, yes. But I try not to think much of it. Worrying will get us nowhere."

"I suppose you're right. It's just hard not to worry sometimes, especially now that Samuel's . . . "

"I understand, but it doesn't benefit us in any way to be concerned with what's already happened. We have to keep marching forward."

The screen on the table flicked on with the video from the drone's camera. Ava took the drone controls and flew it slowly around the room, making sure the camera was working properly. She took out another screen and drone to work on and was able to get the camera working with the screen a few minutes later. She repeated the process a couple more times until there were four screens linked to specific drone feeds.

"I'll go to Lunarford to set up the screens," Ava said. "Once they're set up, I'll need you to control the drones and make sure they're working from range."

She handed me the drone controls as she walked out of the room. A few minutes later, she talked to me through the comms station in her workshop, saying she'd contact me again once she was in Lunarford. I set the drone controls down on the table and then sat back down on the chair until Ava contacted me again. As I watched the hands on the clock tick along for some time, the silence in the room felt suffocating. Ava's voice eventually came through the comms station again.

"I'm in Lunarford, getting the screens set up now. It'll be a few minutes."

"Understood. I have the drone controls ready."

Ava spoke again after a few minutes. "They're ready. Try flying one of the drones around the room."

Picking up the drone controls, I flew one of the drones up slowly. After carefully flying it around the room in circles, I landed it carefully back down on the table. I did the same with the other three drones, flying them all around the room and then landing them. I set the controls back down, waiting for Ava to speak.

"They're all working!" Ava exclaimed excitedly.

"Wonderful!" I said. "They'll be ready for the funeral, then?"

"Yes, they'll be ready. I'll fly them above the cemetery and let them hover before the funeral begins. The soldiers who stay behind will be able to watch the funeral. I'll be back in Esterden soon."

I stayed in the workshop, waiting for Ava to return. I looked around at her various projects, bits and pieces of machinery, and scrap pieces. I was amazed at how much Ava could do with what she had, and I could not wait to see what she would do with a proper setup. Freya walked in the room and sat down in a chair near me, not saying anything. Ava walked back inside a few minutes later and sat down by Freya.

"Are the drones ready for the soldiers in Lunarford?" Freya asked.

"I just got back from setting up the screens for them," Ava replied. "They're working. The drones will be ready for the funeral."

"That's good to hear. I'll call the soldiers back tonight, assuming they aren't attacked. We can call the governors then, too, and tell them to be here in the morning."

"What will we do until then? Not like we have much to do around here today," I said.

"We could watch some movies," Ava said. "I have a few discs and a player I saved, and I can hook it up to a screen in here if you'd like."

Freya smiled. "That would be nice."

Ava set up a screen on her table and connected a disc player to it. We spent a few hours watching some old family movies and stand-up sets, which helped clear our minds and keep us calm. It was nice to have times like these every now and then to distract us from the grim reality we were facing. People we cared about were dying, fighting for their lives against a power greater than ours. I'd thought little about how unevenly our power was matched with Krisprelli's and began to feel horrified by it. After some time, I calmed myself down and kept watching the movie.

"Something wrong, Nate?" Freya asked.

"Uh . . . nothing. It's nothing."

Freya hugged me lightly, saying nothing. I think she could tell I was worried, scared about something, but she didn't say so. I felt like maybe she was sometimes scared, too, but she was too strong to admit it, though others might say she was not strong enough. I was scared, deeply, that we would be dead before the war's end, and it was difficult to avoid thinking about it. I just kept focusing on what was playing on the screen, which was still some stand-up from several years ago.

We could distract ourselves as much as we wanted, but it was only stopping us from acknowledging the reality of our situation. We were all scared—of death, of what could happen to us if we were caught—but we wouldn't say anything about it. We put on a strong facade so everyone around us would not be concerned, and it seemed to work. But internally, I think we were all afraid of the future.

"It's all going to be okay, Nate," Freya said suddenly.

"Wh-what? What do you mean?"

"The war, the Opposition, all of us. I can tell you feel worried, even scared. You aren't hiding it too well."

"I—I . . . thank you, Freya. I think I needed to hear that."

We spent a few more hours watching a couple more movies, which helped ease my mind somewhat. Freya was an empathetic person, so it did not surprise me that she could tell I was afraid of something. Maybe she was right, and maybe everything would turn out okay soon enough. But how soon would that be? How much longer would we suffer? How many more people would we kill and how many more of our people would be killed before we could declare peace?

"That was the last disc," Ava said, digging through the box. "Guess we need to do something else now."

"What time is it right now?" Freya asked

I looked at the clock. "5:57."

"So, we've spent . . . nine hours today watching old stand-up bits and movies meant for children."

"That's right, yes."

"Aren't we in a war?" Ava said. "I feel as if there are better uses of our time than this."

"That's also right," I said.

"We should call the soldiers back soon," Freya said. "It's a decently long ride from Lunarford to here."

I stood up from my seat. "Let's call them back at 7:00. If Krisprelli hasn't sent in any forces by then, he won't be sending any."

"Agreed. I'll give them the call in an hour. How should we decide who stays behind?"

"The soldiers who were assigned into group four during the standoff," I said. "They should be the ones who stay behind to defend."

"Why them specifically?" Freya asked.

"They were the strongest fighters, and there are four snipers in the group. They're the most logical group to leave behind in terms of the actual soldiers assembled there."

"Understandable. I'll give them the call in an hour, then."

"We should call the governors," Ava spoke up. "Shouldn't we?"

"Yes, we should," I replied, and we walked to the surveillance room.

I started a call to the governors, and Marie picked up. "Hey, guys, what do you need?"

"Samuel's funeral will be tomorrow morning," I answered. "We would appreciate it if you would tell everyone else."

"Of course! What time should we get there?"

"Early morning. We don't have an exact time yet. We'll just be glad to see you in attendance."

"We'll all be there to pay our respects. Thank you, Nate. Have a good night."

"You, too, Marie."

The call clicked off then, leaving Freya, Ava, and me in silence for some time. We decided to stay in the room, as Freya would need to come back anyway to call the soldiers later. We sat around, looking at one another but not saying much. Ava flew one of the drones around above Lunarford but saw nothing, which was a good thing. About half an hour passed before one of us broke the awkward silence.

"Going to be a lot of people around here tomorrow," Freya said.

"They'll all be here for Samuel," I said. "I still can't quite believe he's gone."

"We'll all miss him, Nate. In time, we'll all be able to forgive him."

"Some of us already have," I admitted quietly.

"I'm sure he'd appreciate hearing that."

We sat for several more minutes in the surveillance room until it hit 7:00, and Freya called the troops back to base. She told group four they'd be staying behind, and they had no objection to it. They stuck to their duty as their commander had ordered them. Ava, Freya, and I walked to the barracks and waited for the soldiers to return so we could welcome them back to base, if only for tonight and the next morning. We all returned to our rooms afterward.

I lay in bed, drifting in and out of sleep, trying to think of what I would say tomorrow. The funeral would be attended by hundreds of Opposition members, all of them paying their respects to the friend we had lost. I thought about that as I fell into sleep.

CHAPTER EIGHTEEN

I awoke early the next morning, not letting my nightmares slow me down, and put on the only nice set of clothes I had to get ready for the funeral. Sitting down at my desk, I took a few minutes to consider what I would say at the funeral. I was sure several of us would deliver speeches, but I wanted to be sure I had some idea of what I would say. After a little while, Ava came into my room.

"The governors are here in case you want to talk to any of them before the funeral."

"I'll be out there shortly. Thank you, Ava."

Ava walked out of my room and continued on her way. I spent just a few more minutes thinking over my words before I left my room. The noise at the base was louder than I'd heard in quite a few days, not incredibly loud but noticeable. I made small talk with several people as I walked throughout the hallways, trying to find the governors. I was able to find them after a few minutes, all gathered together in a group.

Sylvestor shook my hand as I walked up. "Hello, Nate. Good to see you again."

"Good to see you, too. Thank you for coming."

"We wouldn't have missed this for anything," Marie spoke up. "We all wanted to pay our respects to Samuel."

"It's been a difficult time for us," I said. "Samuel was a good friend, even considering his actions."

"May he rest in peace," Cassius said.

We were all silent for a moment, paying respects to Samuel. It would be difficult for all of us to move past his death. I kept quiet slightly longer than the governors did. Ava walked over to us a few minutes later.

"The service is starting in half an hour," Ava said. "You should all be ready."

Cassius finished his water. "Thank you, Ava. I'll be out there in just a moment."

Cassius would be the priest for Samuel's funeral. He did not mind performing the task. He walked away from us a few minutes later, going to the cemetery grounds to be ready for the funeral. The other governors and I kept talking for a few more minutes but not about much of anything. Freya joined us eventually.

"Freya," Marie said, "how is your recovery going?"

"About as well as it could be. Still wearing these robot legs."

"Well, hopefully, you won't need them much longer."

Freya and Marie kept talking until it was nearly time for the funeral to start. The governors, Ava, Freya, and I made our way to the cemetery, where Samuel's casket was already sitting on the stone pedestal, flowers on top of it. I walked forward and placed more flowers on it, and Freya and Ava then did the same. We took our seats, and the governors sat near us. The other Opposition members joined us a few minutes later, and Cassius began the service.

"Dearly beloved, we're gathered here to pay our respects to our friend Samuel Dakota. His death was caused by the regime of Krisprelli. May his soul rest in peace. If anyone would like to say a few words, please come up."

I walked up to the podium and began speaking. "Samuel was a good man, a good friend, and a great member of the Opposition. He was killed—I killed him." My voice wavered, but I took a deep breath and continued. "He betrayed the Opposition—forced to by Krisprelli—and he attacked us. Krisprelli has taken so many people from us, and our fight will not return them to us, but it will avenge their deaths—even Samuel's."

I stepped down from the podium, as I could barely stand to say anything more. That was the first time everyone knew why Samuel was killed. There was no immediate reaction, no large response. It hit everyone slowly as they took in the fact that Samuel was working against us. And knowing that I was the one to kill him—it was hard for all of us to really accept, but we all had to.

Ava walked up to the podium next. "Samuel might have done things to harm us, and he was working for Krisprelli, but the fact is that he was forced to do so. He was protecting his son, the person taken from him. I think any of us would do anything to get back the loved ones we've lost, wouldn't we? Maybe we can't forgive Samuel, and that's understandable, but we should remember the good he did for us rather than what he did against us. We should let his death inspire us to fight even harder to stop Krisprelli and end this war."

Ava stepped down from the podium and returned to her seat. It wasn't often that she spoke so passionately, but whenever she did, it was always wonderful to hear. She didn't want anyone to feel disdain or hatred toward Samuel for what he did, and she made sure everyone knew that. A few minutes went by quietly before Freya went up to the podium.

"There's not much I can say that hasn't already been said, but nevertheless, I'll give my speech. Samuel cared about all of us, even in the end. Even when he was actively plotting against us, he still cared about us. He truly did not want to hurt us, let alone cause our deaths, but he did not want to see his son killed, either. He was caught in a trap laid by a most devious man, and he had no way out that would not result in pain. He did what he had to, and it killed him in the end. We'll miss him dearly. May he rest in peace."

Freya returned to her seat after finishing her speech, and everyone was silent for a moment. If Samuel could see the funeral, he'd likely ask why everyone was there for him, of all people, or why everyone was crying for him. He had cared about all of us, but he had never been sure why we cared about him at the same time. Cassius stepped back up to the podium a few minutes later.

"Samuel's burial will occur soon for those who wish to see it."

Ava, Freya, and I got up from our seats and walked to where the casket was, where Cassius, Marie, and Lawrence joined us. We all picked up the casket with care and carried it to where Samuel would be buried, his gravestone already in place. While the Opposition members watched, we lowered the casket carefully into the grave. I could even see the senators in the crowd, which raised my spirits just slightly. We shoveled the soil back into the hole that had been dug for the casket and then smoothed it down.

Freya set the shovel down carefully. "It still doesn't feel quite real."

"It really doesn't," I said. "I keep hoping I'll wake up from some dream, but . . . "

"Krisprelli will pay for this. We'll all work to ensure that," Ava said resolutely.

We went back to base after the burial and sat down with the governors to speak of various topics before building up to more serious matters. It was nice to have a few minutes to clear my mind, however. We eventually got to the topic of our future plans, and Freya began to lay out detailed plans for going farther into Krisprelli's territory. It seemed she had already planned out all our actions between now and the end of the war.

"Right now, we're in Wealdsey, but we'll have control of the state soon enough, as it seems Krisprelli has given up on it. I'll send forces to the city of Oakstone to look for Aleksei."

Marie interrupted Freya. "The governor? He's still alive?"

"He's been sending us letters through our underground couriers. We've been waiting to retrieve him until it is safe to leave Lunarford, which is now."

"Send your people to retrieve him tomorrow," Marie said. "Bring him to Highborough."

"I'll send them out first thing tomorrow morning. They're on their way back to Lunarford right now."

"And," Sylvestor said, "what are our plans after we've officially taken Wealdsey?"

"After Wealdsey, we'll be targeting Hampkurth," Freya said. "It'll be heavily defended, and the fight won't be easy, but once we've taken Hampkurth, it won't be long before we can march on Krisprelli's hold and end this war."

"As long as we're getting closer to ending Krisprelli's life, any plan is fine with me," Sylvestor added.

"We need to be getting back to Highborough soon," Margaret said suddenly. "We still have work to get done."

Sylvestor stood up. "Yes, of course. It's been good talking with you all. Hopefully, we can be back again soon enough."

The governors all stood up, got in the truck that had brought them to the base, and rode back to Highborough. It was not a very far distance, but they were busy people and had work to attend to. Ava, Freya, and I went to the planning room and sat down. Freya took out a map and spread it across the table. It was the same map she used when she was planning our march to Wealdsey.

Freya drew various paths across the map. "If our soldiers make it to Oakstone and bring Aleksei into Opposition territory uncontested, I say we can declare Wealdsey as firmly Opposition-held territory."

"I agree," I said, "but what will we do afterward? We can't immediately launch another attack on Krisprelli's territory. Our people will need time to rest; the injured will need time to recover. We need to make sure Aleksei is safe and uninjured."

"Yes, of course. We'll allow the soldiers time to rest and the injured time to heal for a few days. I'll need to create a detailed battle plan beforehand as well. Once everything's in place, we'll begin the fight for Hampkurth as we march closer to Krisprelli."

"Understood. I'm going to go back to my room. I need some rest."

"I'll talk with you more later, Nate."

I went back to my room and lay down on my bed. The day had been mentally and emotionally exhausting for me, so it was quite nice to have a moment of rest. It felt like the end of the war was so close yet so immeasurably far away at the same time. How much longer would it be until I could once again have a proper night of rest—a night unbothered by the images of death that plagued me?

I finally fell asleep and awoke the next morning to see my comms station blinking with a message from Freya. She asked me to go to the planning room, so I tidied myself up and headed in. Ava was already sitting inside when I entered, and I sat beside her.

Freya was pacing around the room for a minute before she said anything. "Our soldiers are going toward Oakstone right now. They'll search for Aleksei once they get there and then bring him to our base when they find him."

"And if they can't find him?" Ava asked.

"They will. One of our couriers picked up a letter from him in Oakstone yesterday. He'll still be in the city and safe."

"What are they bringing him back here for? Why not take him to Highborough with the other governors?" I asked.

"Ava wanted to look at any injuries he may have, and I figured it may be good to ask him a few questions. Once we're sure he's completely okay, we'll take him to Highborough with the rest of the governors."

We waited for around an hour until we heard word from the soldiers in Oakstone. They had found Aleksei and were bringing him back to base. About an hour later, one of our trucks dropped off Aleksei, and two of our soldiers brought him to us. With him in safety, it meant Wealdsey could officially be declared Opposition territory. We would call the soldiers back to base later, but for now, we had questions for Aleksei.

CHAPTER NINETEEN

Aleksei had some small cuts and bruises across his body, which Ava inspected and treated as well as she could. We offered him a cup of tea, and, in turn, he asked for whiskey. Aleksei shifted uncomfortably, but once he had some time to rest in a calm place such as our base, he'd likely feel more comfortable talking with us. He quickly drank the small glass of whiskey Freya gave him and straightened up in his seat. We gave him a few more minutes before we started our questions.

"How long were you pinned down in Oakstone?" I asked.

"Krisprelli's forces had already been patrolling the state since before the war began, but they became more aggressive after the attack in Highborough," he said. "Your launching the attack on Lunarford did make it a bit safer for me, but I was still trapped."

"Why didn't you leave with our couriers whenever they retrieved your letters? It should have been safe to go with them."

"It's actually not all that safe for our couriers," Freya said. "They're usually injured along their routes, and they wear armor. Aleksei actually made the smarter decision by staying behind until our soldiers got to him."

"It feels good to finally be out of that town," Aleksei said while pouring himself another whiskey. "Hopefully, I'll be able to return to it soon enough without worrying about those Royal Army bastards."

Freya pulled out a map. "Do you know of any open paths into Hampkurth from Wealdsey? Maybe something secret that the Royal Army wouldn't know about?"

"Secret paths into Hampkurth? Hmm . . . no, don't know anything about anything like that. If any did exist, the Royal Army would likely know about them, anyway. They likely would have been the ones to dig them."

"I'll keep scouting for other openings into the state, then," she said. "Thank you."

"I don't mean to be rude, but is there a proper bed I could sleep on somewhere? Sleeping on the floor in Oakstone for as long as I had to wasn't exactly the most pleasant thing I've done."

"I'll take you to one of the empty rooms," Ava said as she stood up. "Follow me."

Ava walked out of the room, Aleksei following close behind. Freya was still looking at her map, reviewing the various paths leading into Hampkurth. She was always looking for an opening, planning our next moves, thinking through different strategies and tactics, her mind never ceasing. We had to constantly be moving to have a chance against Krisprelli. If we stagnated too long, he would gain the upper hand and crush us in one decisive strike. Our progress was incredibly slow, while Krisprelli could destroy us and end all of this in one day if he decided to.

Maybe he thought of it like a game, one where he would build us up to win, only to execute a move in our blind spot that would cause everything to come crashing down and leave us burning in the wreckage. Perhaps Krisprelli hadn't thought that far ahead and was simply fighting the war as it came to him with little forethought. That may not be a great surprise to me due to his actions before the war began and how increasingly unstable he had become since then. Was our enemy an unstable madman with no plan, or was he a twisted genius who planned out his every measure and movement beforehand?

"It'll be a few days before I have all the plans in order," Freya said, still inspecting her map. "It should give the soldiers plenty of time to return to base and rest before they have to go back out."

I picked up a cup of tea. "What should we be doing in the meantime?"

"Resting, enjoying ourselves, such as we can in our current situation. Make the best of what we have here until we can return to life as it was before the war."

"Both of us know we'll not be able to return to our lives from before. We'll be expected to take up positions of power, we'll be written into history books, and our names won't be forgotten in Walneyria for quite some time, even after we're gone."

"We can worry about that once we've gotten to that point, Nate. We'll live in the base as we have been, and we'll keep progressing into enemy territory to take it for the Opposition until eventually we've taken everything we can from Krisprelli, attacked his hold, and taken his miserable life from him. We'll make him pay for his actions, and then we'll declare Walneyria ours once more."

"It won't be that easy—it can't be that easy. It'll be a difficult, treacherous path to Krisprelli, with the final roadblock being every soldier he has at his disposal. We'll be powerless to fight against a full-on battle against them. We'll be pinned down from all sides as they close in on us."

"Thoughts like that will get us nowhere, Nate. We need to keep planning, keep moving forward. If we keep the pressure on Krisprelli and his army, we'll be able to push through in time."

"We've been able to push through the smaller states easily enough, sure, but it won't be as easy to get close to Krisprelli's hold. He likely already stations 90 percent of his troops there, and once we get close, he'll call in every possible member of his army to fight us. We would be trapped in an incredibly uneven fight that would almost definitely kill us."

"We have to keep progressing, no matter the risk," Freya said urgently. "I'll evaluate my plans further and decide what is best for us going forward. For now, maybe some rest would do you good."

"Rest? I've barely been up any time at all. Why would I need to rest now?"

"It just seems like maybe you haven't gotten a good night of rest in a while. Just an hour's sleep may be good."

Freya was only looking out for my health, but it seemed as if she did not want to talk with me much more at that moment. I did not doubt her ability for planning; she'd proven herself several times in that regard. What worried me was the speed at which she wanted to rush forward into battle. If we kept marching forward at full speed, we'd reach a point where we aren't ready for a fight while we are already in the middle of one. I went back to my room and lay in bed, falling asleep before I realized it.

Waking up a few hours later, I felt at least somewhat more rested than I had earlier. I stayed in bed for a few minutes, struggling with the decision to actually get up. Minutes later, I walked over to my desk, wrote down my concerns in a notebook, and then put it back on the shelf. As I left my room, I saw Freya struggling with Samuel's office door before she turned away and walked back to the planning room. I went to the office door and tried to open it, but it was still locked.

Aleksei walked into the hall a few minutes later and, after seeing me messing with the door, went back into his room and came out with a small bag. Kneeling in front of the door, he took out a set of lockpicking tools. He pulled out a few of them and started picking the lock on the office door.

"How'd you learn to do that?" I asked.

"There are a lot of things I had to learn when I was younger. I didn't exactly live the most respectful life in my earlier years. Never mind that, though. What's in this room?"

"It was the office of . . . a friend—a friend who died as yet another casualty caused by Krisprelli. Another death that will be paid for with Krisprelli's blood, but it will never be equivalent."

"No payment will ever equal the lives of our dead, but Krisprelli's body will be a nice token in any case."

Freya came back into the hall, noticing Aleksei and I near Samuel's open office door. She pushed past us and went inside, looking around in cabinets and drawers until she found what she was looking for—Samuel's notebook and briefcase. Freya set them aside and kept looking around the room but found nothing else of great importance. I stepped inside before she completely ruined the room.

"What are you looking for exactly?" I said as I stopped her from pulling out another drawer.

"Nothing in particular, other than those," she said, pointing to the notebook and briefcase.

The notebook's cover was clear now, and I could see what was stamped on it: "Royal Army Field Book, issue to Samuel Dakota." Samuel was never part of the Royal Army, of course, but Krisprelli gave him the notebook. The briefcase was locked with no hint of the combination. I gave it to Aleksei, who had it unlocked in a very short time. Freya walked to my side as I opened the briefcase and removed its contents.

Another notebook, this one smaller with no remarkable features, a map of Walneyria with nothing obvious marked, and a small light. Freya took the map and pinned it on the wall, plugging the light into a nearby outlet. The light illuminated the map, revealing hidden ink that showed a network of underground tunnels crisscrossing underneath Walneyria.

We stared at the map for a few seconds, its meaning slowly dawning on us. "There are secret tunnels!" Freya exclaimed.

"They're quite intricate, too," Aleksei said. "Perhaps they were being dug before the war began."

I inspected the map more closely. "They were definitely dug before the war started. They led to Opposition territory, and there's no way the Royal Army could have dug them into our territory after the start of the war without our knowing it."

"What was the use of these tunnels, then? How long have they existed?"

"It's likely they were used for transport," Freya said. "Maybe smuggling? The underground tunnels would have allowed for faster travel between cities. No major landmarks or large crowds to slow down passage. Smugglers using the tunnels could have brought products to customers across the country."

Aleksei stepped closer to the map. "They're miles-long underground tunnels that people were traveling through on foot. They would have needed light, food, water, places to set up a warm shelter. It seems like a lot of work for transporting and smuggling materials."

"There was good money to be made from smuggling back in the day." Freya smirked. "But the important thing here is the fact that Samuel had this map and the light to reveal the tunnels. He was using them to move between here and Krisprelli's hold without our seeing him."

"We could take those tunnels directly to Krisprelli's hold, then?" Aleksei asked.

"The answer to if we *could* is yes," Freya answered. "If we *should*, however, is a definite no. The Royal Army definitely knows about these tunnels if Krisprelli gave Samuel a map of them. They'd no doubt be guarding the exit to them that leads into the hold. It would be incredibly dangerous, and we would be fools to seriously consider it."

"What will we do, then?"

"I'm getting plans ready for fighting in Hampkurth, but it'll be a few days. We'll need to call the soldiers back to base to allow them some rest. Could you do that, Nate?"

I walked up to the surveillance room, giving the soldiers the order for every one of them to return to base. I heard a few small cheers and words of excitement from the troops as they boarded the vehicles. It would be an hour or so before they were back, so I returned to Samuel's office with Freya and Aleksei. They were still inspecting the map and the tunnel paths. I picked up one of Samuel's notebooks, the smaller, unremarkable one. The first few entries were of little interest, written before he had even come in contact with the Opposition. It wasn't until the sixth entry in the journal that he mentioned joining a rebel group. Then, several entries discussed what we were doing and how he had been contributing, somewhat interesting but nothing major. Entry 17 was rather interesting, however. That was the entry when Samuel wrote about his son being taken, about Krisprelli forcing him to work for him. There were a few more entries in the journal, all of them the depressing words of Samuel pleading for his son back.

I could barely stand to read it and threw it back in the briefcase as I moved to his other notebook, the one with the Royal Army insignia on the front. The various entries described Samuel's plans, the intricacies of his plots, and when he was intending to set them in motion. Other entries were written transcripts of his meetings with Krisprelli. Reading it filled me with a sense of dread, and I put it back on the desk.

"I'll be leaving for Highborough in the morning," Aleksei said as he left the office. "Gonna go be with the rest of the governors."

Aleksei's personality seemed unusually calm and carefree, but I thought little of it. Maybe it was simply an outward appearance to hide his fears. Freya unpinned the map from the wall and carefully rolled it up, taking the light with her as she went back to the planning room. I went to the barracks by myself, welcoming the soldiers back once they returned, and retired to my room for a few minutes.

Lying in bed, I thought about what I read in the notebooks. Samuel was an impressive writer, and the entries he wrote after Krisprelli took his son nearly caused me to cry. Samuel was in pain, longing to protect the son Krisprelli took from him. Reading through the other notebook showed the remorse he felt for going against the Opposition and showed how far he would go to protect his son. I missed him greatly and thought of him only as a friend, not a traitor, in this moment. But sometimes that other feeling crept up, and my brain would say nothing except that Samuel was a traitor. I battled with my thoughts until exhaustion won out.

CHAPTER TWENTY

S tepping into the hallway the next morning, I saw Aleksei walking out the front door and getting into one of our trucks so someone could drive him to Highborough. I went back to Samuel's office, grabbed the notebook and briefcase, took them back to my room, and hid them under the bed. I wouldn't read them again, but I wanted to keep them safe for the future. Heading to the planning room, I found Freya investigating the map of the tunnels.

"The Royal Army could move through these tunnels easily," Freya said as she traced the paths with her finger. "They could set up an ambush and attack us, and we'd have no way of knowing."

I thought for a moment. "We could seal the tunnel exits, couldn't we? We have this map, after all."

"We could, yes. It looks like there are four exits in Opposition territory—one in Swindance, one in Lunarford, one in the city of Simontown in Yellowbend, and the last one in Stillburg in Wood-hollow."

"We just need to find the exits and seal them, then," I said. "We could use concrete and metal sheets. If the Royal Army tries to get through them, they'd make too much noise for us not to know."

"Give me a minute," Freya said. "I'll try to overlay this map with the regular map of Walneyria to see exactly where the exits are." Freya took her map of Walneyria and put it on top of the tunnel map. The regular map was semitranslucent and we could see the tunnel's paths clearly underneath. Freya carefully looked at the map and recorded the latitude and longitude of the exits that were in Opposition territory. We'd spend most of the day going around sealing up the tunnel exits, but it was necessary for our safety.

Freya rolled up the maps and put them away carefully. "Ava still has a few sheets of the alloy she used for armor plating lying around. If we put them with concrete mix, we'll have what we need to seal the exits."

"We should ask her to come with us. Any help would be good to have."

Freya and I walked out of the planning room and went to Ava's workshop where she was working on a small scavenged bit of tech. I sat down while Freya gave Ava a hug and looked at what she was working on. Ava didn't say anything and kept working for a few more minutes before she turned around and put down what she was working on.

"What do you guys need?" Ava asked as she sat down.

"Some of the alloy sheets," Freya replied, "the ones you used for the armor. And some concrete mix, if you have any."

"Yeah, I have those. What are we doing with them?"

"We found a map of hidden tunnels under Walneyria," Freya said. "We need to seal the exits in Opposition territory to prevent the Royal Army from using them to ambush us."

Ava was taken aback for a moment but then busied herself gathering the materials. She walked into a small storage room off her workshop and came back out with alloy sheets, bags of concrete, and a welding tool. Freya called for a truck at the front entrance, and once it arrived, we all helped load the materials. It was an uninteresting drive to Swindance, and once there, we grabbed a few of the alloy sheets, bags of concrete, and the welding tool and asked the driver to wait for us.

Freya was looking at a small GPS device, checking for the latitude and longitude she had recorded as the tunnel exit. It took us several minutes of searching, but eventually we found the entrance to the tunnel—a large, metal door, rusted and overgrown with bushes. It obviously hadn't been used in quite some time. With a bit of effort, Ava was able to pull it open.

I grabbed a bag of concrete and began mixing it. "Is it really worth the time to seal this? It looks like this door hasn't been touched in years."

"You're right," Freya said, grabbing another bag, "but we should still seal it, just to be safe."

We spent some time mixing together concrete and pouring it into the hole until there was enough to prevent access to the tunnel. Ava took a few of the alloy sheets and welded them over the door into a thick layer. It would be nearly, if not actually, impossible to open the door from the inside. We went back to the truck and began the ride to Lunarford.

"How long have these tunnels been here?" Ava asked. "That door looked like it has been in place since I was a child."

"It's not unlikely. It actually could have been there since you were a child, and probably before then. There was a lot of smuggler activity going on in Walneyria during the 1990s. The tunnels likely weren't dug by the smugglers, but it wouldn't be surprising if they made use of them."

"They were dug in the 1950s," our driver spoke up. "They were going to be used for a tram system, but that never happened."

"Tuesday Revolt?" I asked.

"Tuesday Revolt. The revolt actually stopped quite a few public works projects. The tunnels were known to be a hangout for smugglers and other criminals. The entrances were covered up, and the government hid their existence after a while. Where'd you get the map of them, anyway?"

"Samuel had it. Given to him by Krisprelli so he could move in secret, out of our view."

"Ah, should have known Krisprelli would utilize the tunnels. Makes sense why you're sealing them, then."

The rest of the ride to Lunarford was fairly quiet as none of us had much more to say. We grabbed our materials, and Freya used her GPS to find the tunnel door. It was easier for us to find the door in Lunarford than the one in Swindance since it was not as heavily rusted or overgrown. Strangely, it seemed as if someone had been caring for it.

Ava knelt down by the door. "Perhaps Samuel was using this door to go between our base and Krisprelli's hold."

"Perhaps," I answered, "but he could not have used it the entire time he was going between Esterden and Krisprelli's hold. We had already been fighting in Lunarford before his death."

"Maybe he was using the door in Swindance in his last few days," Freya suggested. "We did see him going toward Goldheart that day he took down the drone."

"Possibly. He wouldn't have had much time to clean up that door if that were the case."

Ava pulled open the tunnel door, much more easily than she had opened the door in Swindance. Once again, we mixed up several bags of concrete and poured them into the entrance until it blocked the door. Then Ava welded alloy sheets over it, sealing it closed. We went back to the truck and set off toward Simontown.

"Maybe once the war's over, we can actually use the tunnels for the tram system they were dug for," our driver said as we got into the truck.

I thought about it for a moment. "Maybe we can. It'll be quite some time before we have the chance to even consider that, though."

"You could probably find some interesting things in those tunnels if you looked through them," added the driver.

"Like what?" Freya asked.

"Things left behind by people who used to hide out in them. Nothing incredibly valuable but definitely interesting things."

"Hmm. Maybe we'll look through them after the war," I said. "It would definitely be interesting to find things left behind from that long ago."

We were in Simontown a few minutes later and repeated what we had done the last two times. Freya used her GPS to find the door, yet again another rusted, overgrown one. The rust on this one had gotten so bad that holes scattered across it. Freya forced the door open, and we mixed together concrete once again, pouring it into the hole to block it. Ava welded the door shut with the metal sheets, and we went back to the truck, beginning the ride to Stillburg.

"Next door's the last one, right?" the driver asked.

"Yes, it is," Freya answered.

"Going back to base afterward?"

"Yes, we are."

The rest of the ride went along quietly, and we were in Stillburg soon enough. We grabbed the last of our supplies and found the door, once again rusted and overgrown. We repeated the process we had used for the last three doors and returned to the truck. Once back at the base, we returned to the planning room.

"Now that we have those tunnels sealed," Freya said as she took out her map, "we can focus on our plans for Hampkurth."

"Yes. What have you come up with for what we'll do there?" I asked.

"There are two major cities in Hampkurth: Blackacre and Porton. If we take those, we'll have a hold on the state. Krisprelli may fight hard to take them back, but as long as we can defend them long enough, we'll take the state."

"And Zoe Korenz? What about her?"

"We'll find her and bring her into our custody," Freya said. "We can question her and use her to bargain with Krisprelli if the opportunity were to occur."

"And what will we do after we take Hampkurth?"

"I'll need to evaluate the openings we would gain from taking the state and determine the best course of action for us to act on."

"Understood. In the meantime, what should we be doing?"

"The soldiers should be resting," Ava spoke up, "and we should be preparing. We're the leaders of this group, after all. We need to be ready for everything so our people can be inspired by us."

Freya seemed surprised by Ava's words and took a minute before she spoke again. "Y-yes, that's right. We need to be preparing our future actions; we need to be ready. I'll keep working on my battle plans so they can be ready once the soldiers have rested. Ava can keep working on her tech, and Nate, you can help us."

"It seems a bit rude that I don't have a specific job, but also entirely understandable," I said.

"We'll need to be ready to fight again soon. We have to keep the pressure on Krisprelli."

"For how much longer, though? How much longer will this fighting continue, Freya?"

"None of us knows the answer to that, Nate. We'll fight until we've won the war; we'll fight until we get to Krisprelli and kill him. We'll fight until we physically can't keep fighting any longer."

I began to feel a growing sense of panic.

"We'll end this war soon," Ava said suddenly. "I know it. We'll get to Krisprelli and make him pay for what he's done to us. We have to."

"Definitely," Freya replied. "Krisprelli has to pay for what he's done to this country, for everyone and everything he's taken from us. We'll end this war and end Krisprelli."

Freya and Ava were determined and sounded very sure of what they said. We would make Krisprelli pay, but would it really be soon? The closer we got to Krisprelli, the end seemed even farther away. It was difficult for us to keep going, to keep fighting. We gave everything we had to the Opposition, and, in turn, we were paid with pain delivered by Krisprelli's soldiers.

I ran out of the planning room and rushed to my bed, trying to abate the panic spreading throughout my body.

CHAPTER TWENTY-ONE

My mind tormented me, giving me not even a moment's respite as it continually assaulted my senses. The walls I had built around me to protect myself came crashing down, leaving me vulnerable. In that moment, every feeling, every emotion, every sense was stripped from me, except for one: panic. An intense, searing panic enveloped my mind and drained away safety and security. It ate away at me, breaking down my mental faculties until I only felt an intense, growing dread.

Ava came into my room and handed me a small cup of liquid. I did not ask what it was and simply drank it. The taste was foul, and I barely managed to swallow the fluid as it entered my mouth. I felt my senses lightening somewhat, returning to normal, before I fell unconscious. Sometime later, I awoke, Ava still standing by my bed.

I sat up in my bed. "Wh-what was that? How long was I out?"

"Something to help you calm down," Ava answered. "We were incredibly concerned when you ran out of the room like that. As for your state of consciousness, you were only asleep for about three minutes. You should be all right now, though."

"I . . . I don't know what happened to me. Everything started feeling . . . wrong, off in some way. I got scared, for lack of a better word."

"It sounds like you had a panic attack. Reasonable, considering the situation. That liquid I gave you should help keep you calmed down, at least for a little while."

"Thank you, Ava. How are Freya's plans coming along?"

"Well, again, it's only been a few minutes since you ran out of the room, so she hasn't really made much progress."

"Ah, yes. Sorry, perception of time's a bit off right now. Give me a few minutes."

"Just rest for now, Nate. You don't need to be working too hard right now."

"Weren't you saying how all of us need to be preparing? What use am I if I'm laid up in bed because my mind is acting poorly?"

"Nate," Ava said sternly, "you need to rest. Just for a few hours so you can calm down. You'd be equally useless with your mind acting at a fault as you would be resting in here."

"Okay, okay. I'll stay in here, stay out of your way."

"You know it wasn't meant like that, Nate."

I smiled. "I know. Go on. I'll rest in here while everyone else goes about their business."

"I'll be in my workshop. Come talk to me once you feel a bit better."

"I will. Thank you, Ava."

"Oh! Before I go," Ava said as she pulled out a vial from her pocket, "here's more of the medicine I gave you, in case you need it again."

Ava set the vial down on the table by my bed and left my room. I lay in bed, trying not to think about much in particular. I felt much calmer than I had earlier due to the medicine. Ava had not told me what it was, but at the moment, I didn't particularly care about that. I thought about what we were doing, how much longer we would fight.

I was still worried, even scared, of course, but calmer than I had been earlier. How many more days of fighting would we endure? How many more miles of marching? How much more blood would be shed in the name of the Opposition? To say I was only scared would be an understatement. I was terrified of what we would have to continue to endure before we ended this war. I was terrified that the people I cared for the most—the people who were about the only good friends I had left in this world—would be taken from me, just as everyone else had been. Just as Samuel was taken from us.

Death is an uncaring, soulless being, the fusion of Mortality and Time into one strangling, choking beast. It's an embodiment of terror and sadness that preys on even more terror and sadness. Death devours everything, furthering itself as a monster that roots itself into everyone's souls, tearing them apart until it consumes them entirely. Perhaps I would never see Time or Mortality or Death, not in the ways I personify them, though I wasn't sure I would necessarily want to see them. If I was ever to see them, that would mean they caught up to me, that I lost. I had to be sure that wasn't going to occur anytime soon.

That night, I fell asleep thinking about Death and stayed asleep until the next morning. I drank the vial of medicine Ava left on my table and got out of bed a few minutes later. My movements felt light, as if I had become weightless, and for a moment, I was concerned. Gradually, I once again began to feel the effects of gravity properly as I walked over to my desk and sat down. I grabbed one of my notebooks and started writing in it about my worries, how I was scared about our future. It served as a way for me to let out my emotions without my mind overloading itself with several different responses.

I left my room a few minutes later and went to Ava's workshop. She had fallen asleep in the chair near her worktable, which had various mechanical pieces scattered over it. I sat in one of the other chairs, waiting for her to wake up. I wasn't sure what Ava had been working on, but it was obvious she was working late into the night if she had fallen asleep in her workshop. A few of the pieces on the table looked like limbs for a robot. Not like the legs Ava built for Freya, but rather full limbs that were entirely mechanical. I waited around 20 minutes until Ava woke up.

"Oh, hey there, Nate," Ava said as she awoke. "What time is it?"

"9:32, morning. What were you working on?"

"Trying to reverse engineer some of these robot arms. If I could work out how the AI chips cause the movements, I could modify its setup to be linked to the human nervous system."

"I thought you'd already made something like that, for the legs for Freya."

"That was just an early design. It's serviceable, but there are several areas where I could improve it. Basing it on some of these AI chips won't completely fix the areas where there are issues, but it would be a good start."

"What needs to be improved? The one you used for the legs seems to work just fine."

"That's exactly it—the one for the legs works, but only just. I need to work on making the connection between the apparatus and the user's mental state stronger, more stable. Make the movements more fluid beyond just refining the physical machinery. I planned to investigate the legs more thoroughly and take them apart once I felt comfortable that Freya did not need them anymore. She's already healed pretty well, but the legs are still helpful for now."

"Would you even have the resources here to build something like that? It sounds like it would be a rather difficult project to actually construct."

"I barely have the resources to reverse engineer the AI chips I have here. I would not even get close to constructing neural interface chips, but having the initial research is the main goal. I'll worry about the actual construction of the device after the war is over and I can perform my work in a lab that's lit by more than flickering lights and a single small window."

"I see. How is your research going so far, then?"

She reached for a tool I didn't have a name for. "So far, not incredibly well. I've managed to write down the general layout and actual construction of the AI chip, but its coding, power requirements, and other dependencies will be more difficult to work out. I need a computer I can slot one of the chips into and get a dump of the code."

"Are there any computers like that somewhere?"

"There are, in Krisprelli's territory. Hampkurth is a tech center; if there's any place that would have them, it would be somewhere there. We could probably find some other helpful things scattered around, too. Porton was a development hub; they have both research labs and manufacturing plants. We could likely recover some blueprints along with already built pieces of tech."

"If we had access to manufacturing centers," I said, "we could start producing more sets of armor, couldn't we? Maybe we could even get access to the resources you need to build gravity wells into more suits."

"We'll worry about that once we get there, Nate. For now, we should go talk with Freya. See how her planning is coming along."

Ava tidied her worktable slightly as I walked out of the room, and she joined me in the hall soon after. We walked into the planning room where Freya was moving around frantically, looking over several maps, comparing troop movements and placements. She barely seemed to notice Ava and me as we walked in, and we sat down so as not to disturb her. She kept looking over the map for several minutes before she said anything to us.

"It's going to be difficult for us to get into Hampkurth," she blurted out. "On the outskirts of the state there's dense vegetation, and once we get into the state, we'll be fighting in large cities that would afford the Royal Army several places to hide. Our snipers will have several areas of high ground, but so will the Royal Army. I'll need another day of planning. The plan will be ready tomorrow. We'll brief the troops on it and give them the remainder of the day to rest, and they'll go out onto the field the next day. Does that sound good to you?"

"That sounds good," I replied. "The troops will have had enough time to rest, and we won't have been out of battle for too long."

What's the Royal Army's position in the state?" Ava asked.

"When I looked with the drones a few hours ago, there were sizable groups dispatched in Blackacre and Porton. They're the most logical cities for us to attack, and they realize that."

I thought for a moment. "We'll need to be careful getting to the cities, then, staying out of their sight and remaining concealed for as long as possible. If they see us before we are ready, they'll kill as many of us as possible. They have plenty of explosives to throw at us."

"I'll account for stealth in the plans," Freya replied, "and find the best paths to stay hidden. We'll be ready to fight in two days."

"What will we do in the meantime?" Ava asked.

"We'll do what we've been doing. Surviving, doing our work. Everything will be in order before we go back into battle."

The rest of the day passed with little importance. Ava went back to her workshop and kept working on various projects, while Freya continued to plan. I went around the base and talked with a few Opposition members for a few hours and then went back to my room. I read one of my books I had read before since I had exhausted the supply I had. It was late by the time I finished reading it, so I put it back and lay in bed. For once, my mind decided it did not want to torment me while I attempted to sleep.

I woke up early and went to the planning room. Freya was sitting at the table, writing on the map, making the last few adjustments to the plan before it would be ready. I sat down across from her. She glanced up at me and then returned to the map. A few minutes later, Ava came in and sat down. We waited just a bit longer until Freya put away her pen and finished the map.

"We're ready," Freya said.

Ava smiled lightly. "Good. What is the plan?"

"We'll divide our troops into two large groups as equal in size as we can. They'll go through two different points along the border of the state and make their way through the forest. They'll stick to a specific path I've drawn and get close to Blackacre and Porton. The snipers will get to the tops of buildings and begin the fight, the same way we've been doing."

"And once we take the city?" I asked.

"We'll make sure our hold is firm, the troops will return and rest, and we'll return to planning. It's our cycle at that point."

"We need to brief the troops about the plan, then," I said, "and tell them they're going out tomorrow."

Freya got up from her seat without a word and left the room. Ava and I followed her to the barracks where we gathered the troops together. Freya spent several minutes giving the soldiers a detailed outline of the plan and telling them their agenda once they were on the path toward Hampkurth. She finished by telling them they were leaving tomorrow, which the troops responded to rather neutrally. Freya, Ava, and I went back to the planning room.

"Ever closer, we march toward the keep of our enemy," Ava said as she sat down.

"And ever closer do we march toward death at the same time," I replied.

"We'll see what happens in the following days," Freya said. "When we take Hampkurth, it won't be much farther until we get to Krisprelli."

We spent several more hours making conversation, mostly focused on the war and our progress. Later that night, we went back to the barracks and ate dinner with the soldiers before they would leave tomorrow. They didn't seem scared about what they were facing and were proud to be fighting for us. I hoped most of them would be able to return to us after the battle, but there was no way to know until after it was over. We returned to our rooms after a few hours so we would have enough rest for tomorrow.

CHAPTER TWENTY-TWO

I woke up the next morning to a small tray on my desk with a note, a cup of coffee, and a bread roll. I drank the coffee as I read the note. It was from Freya, telling me to come to the planning room whenever I was ready. I sat at my desk for a few minutes longer, finishing the coffee and eating the bread, then hurried off to the planning room where Freya and Ava were already sitting down. I sat in the chair next to Freya.

"Today's the day," Freya said.

"It's just another day," Ava replied. "It won't be the day until we actually get to Krisprelli."

"I suppose you're right about that. But we'll be getting closer to Krisprelli today."

I spoke up after a few minutes had passed. "Even as we get closer, it feels farther away, doesn't it?"

"Sometimes, yes," Ava answered. "Maybe it's the anticipation, the growing intensity as we march closer to Krisprelli's hold."

"Perhaps. I long for the day when we'll be able to stick a knife through that bastard's throat."

Freya spoke up. "Everyone here is anxiously waiting for that day, Nate."

"May it come to us sooner than we expect it, then," I said.

"I would actually prefer it to happen exactly when we expect it. Don't need things happening that go against our plans," Freya said.

"Yes, of course. Let us hope Krisprelli's death happens precisely when we've planned it."

"You always were a bit of a smart ass, weren't you, Nate?"

I smirked. "Guilty."

"Could we be serious for a minute, please?" Ava seemed annoyed.

"Yes, of course. We need to be serious. Today's important," Freya answered.

"Thank you. We need to get the troops ready, don't we?"

"Yes, we should. Make sure they're ready, have their equipment in check, everything of that nature. Maybe Nate can give another speech, too."

"I wouldn't say much different from what I said to them the last time. I'm not exactly a creative person, Freya."

"Any speech is better than none. The troops like hearing you speak. It inspires them!"

"All right, just give me some time to think of what to say."

"You have five minutes. The troops need to head out soon."

We sat in the planning room for the next five minutes. Freya spent the time looking over her maps, and Ava joined her. I thought of what to say, which was difficult given the time constraint placed on me. I decided on something just before the five minutes were up and thought it through a few times. Freya rolled the map up and turned to me.

"You ready?" she asked.

"I . . ."

"It was a rhetorical question, Nate. Let's go."

We walked out of the planning room and went to the barracks where the soldiers were already gathered. A few were in their armor with their other gear ready to go. Most were eating small meals before they would leave the base. Once they finished eating, they got up from their tables, put their armor on, and then got the rest of their equipment ready. We gave them all time to finish their meals and went around helping them with their gear, making sure they had everything they needed. Freya gave a few grenades to some of the soldiers, and I went to the front of the room once everyone was ready.

I cleared my throat and began my speech: "Your fighting in Hampkurth will determine the future of the Opposition as a whole. If—no—when you succeed, we'll take yet another foothold out of Krisprelli's hands, and we'll further weaken his empire. We'll march closer to Krisprelli's hold, closer to the day when we'll end this war. Give them hell! Fight harder than you have yet. Drive them out of Hampkurth. Carry forward the Opposition."

The soldiers clapped, and a few cheered for the speech. I was sure none of them were exactly happy or eager to go out and fight again, but they did it in any case. They had become used to taking lives and seeing the lives of their fellow Opposition members taken. They hadn't become numb to the feeling, but it had become regular for them, enough that it was not difficult for them to continue to go out into enemy territories and kill Krisprelli's men. How many of our own people would lose their lives today, too?

Our troops picked up the bags that held their supplies and climbed in the trucks that would take them to the points on the border where they would enter Hampkurth. We gave them a salute as they drove away and walked to the surveillance room. Ava flew the drones over the trucks and then landed them on top. She would fly them to the cities once our troops made it to their entry points.

"We've all grown so . . . so used to this routine," Freya said. "It's become depressingly regular. It doesn't carry the same feeling of excitement and concern as it did when the war first began. Maybe it's good that battles don't feel as frightening as they used to, but it's upsetting how regular this routine has become."

I thought about her words for a moment. "You're right, Freya. It's become so normal to us that it's hard to feel very concerned about it anymore. We just watch the drone's cameras, watch our troops and

Krisprelli's troops exchange fire, and have our people bring back the dead and injured. It's just routine."

"Soon enough," Ava spoke up, "we'll be able to fall out of this routine and return to our lives before the war—for the most part, anyway."

"Nothing will be the same after the war. You know that, Ava."

"Any life after the end of this war will be good, Nate."

"Assuming we live," Freya said.

"If we were to lose," added Ava, "we wouldn't have a life after the war. Krisprelli would have his troops bring us to him, and he'd execute us. Probably even do it publicly."

"Worrying about that is useless, Ava. For now," Freya said, "we should concern ourselves with ideas of victory. If we keep saying we'll lose, then we'll will it into happening."

"I'm not sure our thoughts have the power to cause something to happen, Freya," I said.

"My point stands. We should worry about victory rather than bring negativity and thoughts of losing."

"I was not saying we would lose," Ava said, annoyed. "Rather, I was saying what would happen if we were to lose."

We sat in silence for a long time afterward as the troops got closer to Hampkurth. Once the trucks stopped, Ava flew the drones up and used them to follow the troops as they marched through the forest. She did not fly them toward Blackacre or Porton just yet. If the Royal Army forces in the city saw them, they would know our troops were approaching. We needed to surprise the RA forces to have an advantage.

"These forests are thick," Freya said. "I'm surprised they weren't cut down for further industrial expansion."

"It was kept so the larger factories in the state wouldn't be as visible in the nearby states," I replied. "Citizens complained. Happened when we were young."

"How'd you know that, Nate?"

"A book on Walneyrian history. One of the few books I was able to recover from our old base."

"You read a history book for fun?"

"Not for fun, Freya, to pass time. It was the only one I hadn't already read recently."

"One day—" Ava hesistated. "—we'll be in a history book, too. Children long after we're dead will learn about us in their classes. Kind of strange to think about that, isn't it?"

"Let's just hope that when we're written into those books, it's not because our side was defeated in the war," Freya replied.

"History is written by the victors," I said. "We just have to be the victors."

"And when we are, we'll write an accurate history, as unbiased as possible, including our losses," Ava added.

"Of course, Ava. Everyone should be able to learn about the history of our country without any spin on it."

"We'll work together with several Opposition members, the governors, and citizens of Walneyria to assemble a comprehensive, accurate, unbiased recollection of the events of the war once it's over."

"I think we will need to sort out the political future of the nation first, and then we can begin to write a history, Ava."

"Of course, Nate. There's going to be quite a lot of work for us to do after the war."

We were quiet again for some time as we continued to watch the troops make their way into the cities. The Blackacre group got into position, with the Porton group doing the same shortly afterward. The ground troops hid behind cover, and the snipers quietly climbed up to the rooftops, taking out any Royal Army snipers on the roof with their suppressed pistols. Freya set the drones to hover above Blackacre and Porton, and she gave the order for the snipers to fire.

As with every battle we had been involved in, our snipers started off by taking out the Royal Army snipers and then picking off any more heavily armored ground troops. Our ground forces fired on the Royal Army troops, taking out several of them. Others threw grenades into groups of RA soldiers, which took out several fighters. Some of the Royal Army focused their fire on one soldier at a time, heavily injuring or killing them by doing so. One threw a grenade into a small group of our people, killing five of them.

"We're losing several people out there," Ava said, sounding worried.

"We can't order a retreat," Freya said, nearly shouting. "They need to keep fighting."

"At least order them to get the injured somewhere where they can treat the wounds! We need to prevent as many deaths as possible."

Freya spoke through the long-range comms, which went through to every soldier, ordering them to get the injured to a safe area so they could give them Sanitatem Celer. Some of our soldiers rushed over to the injured and carried them to cover, treating their wounds as quickly as they could while still making sure they were careful in their work. The number of Royal Army troops in Blackacre had steadily decreased until there were few remaining. Porton, however, was still heavily defended since there had been more of Krisprelli's forces in Porton than Blackacre to begin with.

Freya looked across the screens. "It looks like we'll have Blackacre under our control soon enough. Porton's going to be harder, though I'm not surprised that Krisprelli would fight harder to keep it than Blackacre. Porton has several valuable assets for us once it's ours."

The fighting continued in Blackacre for another half an hour until it was clear of the Royal Army. In Porton, our people continued fighting for several more hours, more of them injured and killed in the process. The Royal Army did not back down. There were fewer of them as time went on, but they continued aggressively, singling out our soldiers to injure them. However, doing so allowed our people to easily find and take out the enemy soldiers. Several more hours passed until it seemed Porton was also clear of the Royal Army.

"We'll just need to hold the cities for a few days," Freya said, "and then Hampkurth will be ours."

CHAPTER TWENTY-TWO

"We're getting close to Krisprelli now," I said.

A few of our people at the base went out to pick up the injured and dead, allowing the soldiers to remain in the cities. After around an hour, they took the dead to the morgue and brought the injured to the medical ward. It seemed like we were done fighting for the day. We began to leave the surveillance room until we heard a loud explosion.

Someone had launched a mortar and hit Porton, killing dozens of our soldiers. Two large groups of Royal Army troops marched toward Porton and Blackacre, shooting hundreds of bullets at our troops. Our snipers picked off some of them, while our troops rushed to cover and began returning fire as the troops approached. The fighting began once again, and more of our people were being killed by the warriors of a twisted man. We weren't even allowed a moment of rest.

CHAPTER TWENTY-THREE

O ur troops fought as hard as they could, shooting several Royal Army soldiers and throwing grenades into larger groups of them. Porton was surrounded by the Royal Army on all sides. In Blackacre, they marched into the center and attacked outward. Our snipers worked as fast as they could to take out some of the soldiers, but our ground forces did most of the work, taking out the larger groups of Royal Army troops. The fighting didn't cease for several more hours, long into the night.

Ava flew the drones around the cities, using their night vision to see everyone who had died. Several of our soldiers were killed, while many more of the Royal Army died in the fighting. Our people tended to the injured and grouped the dead together. Freya told them we'd send a truck to recover them in the morning. The cities weren't safe yet, and they wouldn't be for some time. Krisprelli was fighting with more desperation than ever before since we were getting closer and closer to his hold. For a moment, it seemed like we may have even scared him.

"This is the deadliest battle for our side yet," Ava said. "What are we going to do?"

"We keep fighting until the Royal Army isn't a problem anymore. Then our soldiers come back to base, we plan for a while, and then we go out and fight again. Exactly what we've been doing since the war began," Freya answered sternly.

"But if we keep losing people like this . . . "

"It's war, Ava. People die. People have died. People will die. It's what happens in a war. A war without death would be little more than a large-scale political argument."

"Do you not care about the people we're losing, Freya?"

"I care greatly for everyone who is giving their lives for us. Their deaths bring me great sadness. But I can at least somewhat accept them because it's war."

Ava and Freya turned back to the screens, saying nothing more to each other. I knew Freya did care about those who were killed in action for us, and I understood, too, why she could accept it so readily—because this is a war, and people will die. Ava knew that, but it seemed difficult for her to so readily accept the deaths of Opposition members. Perhaps it seemed Freya was uncaring, that she thought nothing of the deaths we suffered, but that was far from the truth. She'd give her life if it brought back the lives of everyone we lost.

We fell asleep in the surveillance room. It was quite late when the fighting ceased, and we awoke early the next day, the sun having just barely risen. Ava went to the dining hall and came back a few minutes later with coffee and bread for all of us. We consumed our breakfast, such as it was, and then watched the screens once more. Our troops marched through Blackacre and Porton, likely checking for any Royal Army troops.

After several minutes of finding nothing, a group of our people in Porton sneaked up on a small group of Royal Army soldiers, one wounded, the other two treating the injured. Our troops who found them radioed us, asking if they should kill them. It was a difficult question for all of us, and we took several minutes to think it over. Eventually, we decided they could leave them since it was only three people and one was wounded. They were our enemy, sure, but taking the lives of people tending to an injured person seemed brutal.

"They'll never know what we spared them from in that moment," Ava said somberly.

Freya was quiet for a moment. "If they had seen our soldiers, they wouldn't have given a second thought about attacking them."

"The fact that our soldiers hesitated on what would have been easy kills," I said, "is just another sign that we have more empathy than every piece of Krisprelli's regime combined."

Our troops continued to march through Blackacre and Porton, making sure they were secure. They patrolled the city for several hours, watching for any further Royal Army activity, but it wasn't there. We spent most of the day in the surveillance room, watching Blackacre and Porton. After several hours passed, Ava went to the dining hall and brought back another small meal for us.

I ate my meal and then spoke. "It's concerning that no more Royal Army forces have approached the cities today."

"Krisprelli is likely planning," Freya answered, "deciding his next move. He'll probably send more later today, possibly tomorrow."

"Maybe it would be a good idea for us to send some of our troops to find Zoe Korenz and detain her," Ava suggested.

"We could. My intel suggests she's been hiding in Hearncrest, one of the smaller towns in the state. I'll get a few of the soldiers to assemble and send the route to the town to their suits' GPS."

Freya chose a group of 25 soldiers at random and keyed the comms system into their suits specifically. She told them they would be going to find and arrest Korenz, and they responded with a simple "affirmative." Freya pulled out a tablet and uploaded the route to Hearncrest to the GPS in their suits, and they started their march. Ava took control of one of the drones and used it to follow the troops.

It took around 20 minutes for the group to arrive in Hearncrest. Along the path, they ran into small groups of Royal Army soldiers, which they took out easily. Once they got to Hearncrest, they carefully marched around the city, looking for any more of the Royal Army. A large group of Krisprelli's soldiers were gathered inside a church in the town, and our people used their suppressed weapons to take them out. Our troops then went inside the church and investigated it.

"What do you think they should be looking for?" I asked.

"A hidden door," Ava answered, "maybe a hatch of some sort on the floor. Anything that could be used to conceal a room's entrance."

Freya spoke into the comms station again, telling the troops what they should be looking for. Some went to the bookcases, pulling the books off the shelf but finding nothing. Others went to the candle sconces, pulling on them, again finding nothing. One soldier found a loose brick in the wall, but it ended up being just that—a loose brick. Finally, the soldiers moved the large rug that took up a majority of the floor space in the room and found a hatch under it.

At first appearance, the hatch looked old, rusted out, and welded shut. A closer inspection, however, revealed that it was simply made to appear that way. The rust was fake, and the welding was light enough to open. A few of the soldiers worked together to open the hatch and were able to pull it open with enough force. They dropped a light down into the opening and climbed down one by one on the ladder until everyone was inside. Ava carefully maneuvered the drone into the underground room and followed the troops.

The sound of a gunshot filled the room as a bullet hit one of our soldiers in the shoulder. Their armor was able to protect them from injury, and the troops moved forward carefully to the origin of the shot. Someone shot a few more shots as they approached, but they missed. Once the soldiers made it to the corner of the room, they found a woman. One of our people disarmed her and put her in handcuffs.

"Is that Korenz?" Ava asked.

Freya looked closely at the screen. "There's not enough light in the room for a clear enough facial match. I'll need to confirm once the troops are above ground again."

The troops climbed out of the hatch, carrying the woman they had apprehended. When everyone was topside, they shut the hatch. The inside of the church wasn't as dark as it had been underground, but there still wasn't enough light for Freya to see the face of the woman clearly enough to confirm it was Zoe Korenz. The troops carried her outside the church, and all sat down.

"That's Korenz, no doubt about it," Freya said. "We need them to bring her back here immediately."

"What exactly do you want to do with her once she's here, Freya?" I asked.

"Question her, if at all possible. Get any information from her we can, then keep her in one of the cells."

"She will not be quick to just give us information," Ava said. "If she does give up anything, we'll need to take it with a grain of salt. She supports Krisprelli. His supporters are notoriously tight-lipped."

"We'll get what we need from her. I'll make sure of it."

"You aren't implying you'll harm her, are you, Freya?" Ava asked.

"Of course not, but I have my ways of getting people to talk. We'll get Ms. Korenz to tell us what we need to know."

"And," I asserted, "what exactly is it we hope to gain from her? It's not like we need troop movement plans. Krisprelli isn't a tactician, and it doesn't seem he has anyone working for him who is, either."

"He may not have specific battle plans ready beforehand, but he has general ideas, such as sending those groups to Blackacre and Porton."

"I suppose you're right about that, Freya. What else do you want to gain from having her in our custody?"

"We'll use her as a bargaining chip. Try to get something from Krisprelli in exchange for returning her to safety."

"We wouldn't kill her!" Ava exclaimed.

"Of course not, but Krisprelli doesn't know that. If he cares enough about her, he'll give us something in return for her safety. If he doesn't care enough, maybe that will get her to come over to our side."

"We'll discuss that more later," I said. "For now, we should just get her here. Once she's at the base, we'll begin our questions and decide on our further course of action."

"Yes, Nate, you're right. Little use in considering what to do with her before she's even here."

Just then, the video feed from the drones displayed a sight we did not anticipate. Zoe had managed to get out of her cuffs and steal a rifle from one of our people. She focused fire on one soldier, heavily injuring him before she used all the ammo. Two of our people tackled her to the ground and locked her hands into a pair of cuffs that completely covered her hands. They watched her carefully as they marched toward Esterden until one of our trucks picked them up.

Ava flew the drone she had been using to watch the troops back at Blackacre, and we waited for them to get back to Esterden. The ride between Hampkurth and Esterden was not especially long, but it would still be some time before they would be at the base. Ava brought us another small meal from the dining hall, this time tea and a few small cakes.

We ate quietly for a few minutes until Ava spoke. "Are we going to question Korenz immediately?"

"We'll question her tomorrow," Freya answered. "It's getting late now, and we need time to think of exactly what we want to ask."

We finished our meals, and the troops brought Korenz in shortly after. Freya ordered them to take her to one of the cells, which they did, and Freya locked it from a panel in the room. We went back to our rooms for the night to rest. Korenz would be difficult to talk to, and I thought about what I would ask. Perhaps her answers will be exactly what we need.

CHAPTER TWENTY-FOUR

I woke up the next morning to someone knocking loudly on the door to my room. I got out of bed slowly and walked over to the door, opening it to find Freya. She said nothing as she grabbed my hand and pulled me behind her, walking toward Ava's workshop. When we found Ava was not inside, we went to her room and found her. Freya pulled both of us along to the planning room.

"What do you want, Freya?" Ava asked, sounding annoyed.

Freya pulled out some sheets of paper and pens. "Ava, we need to be ready to question Korenz."

"I know that, but what do you want us to do specifically right now?"

"We need to think of some questions and write them down. Gather our thoughts and be prepared for the questioning."

"First," I said, "we'll ask her what Krisprelli's further plans are for Hampkurth, and then we'll ask what his plans are in general. We'll ask if they've been using the tunnels and where Krisprelli stations his troops when they're not fighting."

Freya wrote down what I said. "Is that all?"

"Yes. Those questions should afford us any major information we could possibly need."

"And," Ava spoke up, "we'll need to record a video that says we have Korenz in custody. If I could get one of the Royal Army's suits of armor, I could use it to figure out the broadcast signal they use and utilize it to send the video to every soldier's armor."

Freya spoke into the comms system, asking a few of our people to bring back one of the Royal Army corpses still in Porton. They were confused by the request but did as they were asked. The troops returned some time later, and Ava helped them carry the corpse to her workshop, leaving Freya and me in the planning room by ourselves.

"How are we going to get Korenz to talk?" I asked Freya.

"There are a few chemical compounds that, when administered to someone, make them a bit more . . . pliable to questioning. Their efficacy isn't entirely proven, but they'll help us today."

We left the planning room after a few minutes and went to the workshop. Ava had taken the entire suit of armor from the corpse and put the corpse into a body bag. The armor was damaged in places where gunshots had hit it, but they were mostly scattered on the torso section of the suit. Ava was focusing on the helmet. She pulled a panel off the side of the helmet with some force and revealed a computer chip. Carefully removing the chip, she fit it into a specially modified motherboard, which she then slotted into a computer.

"The chips in these helmets are fairly simple," Ava said as she typed something into the computer. "I can decode them with what I have here with a bit of effort. Getting the radio frequency and upload channel they use should be simple enough."

I sat down. "And what will we do once we have it decoded?"

Freya explained as she stared at the computer screen. "We'll record a video showing we have Korenz here and give a demand to Krisprelli, perhaps the immediate liberation of one of the states he holds or even just sending a governor into our territory. We won't actually harm Korenz, but we'll say that if Krisprelli doesn't give us what we demand, Korenz won't be seen in his territory again."

"Yes," Ava replied. "Then we'll send the video across the broadcast signal for the suits. Every one of Krisprelli's troops wearing their armor at that time will see it."

"We could just demand that he give up Hampkurth," I suggested. Freya thought for a moment. "No, we've already fought for Hampkurth. Getting him to just give it up would be too easy."

"We'll demand Cheson," Ava said, "and the return of the governor, Parker Blackwell."

"And what will we do if Krisprelli doesn't agree to our terms?" I asked.

"We keep Korenz locked in her cell," Freya answered, "and let Krisprelli believe we've killed her, although he likely would care little if we actually did so."

Ava continued working at the computer, decoding the chip from the helmet to find the broadcast signal. Freya and I sat aside and let Ava work in peace while we made small talk. Ava made slight sounds of frustration at times, and it seemed she hit a wall in her work at a few points, but she did not let it slow her down for long. She continued working as quickly and carefully as she could until she turned away from the computer. The screen displayed a completely decoded broadcast frequency we could use to distribute the video.

"It was difficult to get it entirely decoded. Krisprelli had some incredibly qualified people to code this. And my knowledge of programming isn't exactly the best."

"Well, you can't know everything, Ava."

"What I do and don't know is beside the point right now, Nate. What's important right now is the order that we'll be doing this in."

Freya got up. "We record the video first, question Korenz afterward, and then send the video across the broadcast channel for the Royal Army."

"Understood," Ava said, picking up a camera. "Let's go, then. Don't want to waste too much time."

We left the workshop and went down to the cell Zoe Korenz was locked in. Her hands were still cuffed, and she had fallen asleep on the small, stiff bed. Freya unlocked the cell door and went inside, injecting Korenz with a small syringe of a fluid before she could move or resist. Freya then left the cell and locked the door once more. I noticed Zoe slouch over and fall back asleep, the drug apparently already taking effect. Ava asked if we were ready as she set up the camera. Once we gave a signal, she began recording.

"Hello, Royal Army," Freya began, "Krisprelli's loyal lap dogs, and perhaps even Krisprelli himself. We're broadcasting this message to you to tell you we've taken Zoe Korenz, one of your supporters, into our custody. We will return her to you safely if you give us what we demand, the immediate liberation of the state of Cheson to the Opposition States and the return of Cheson's governor, Parker Blackwell, to our lands. If you do not give us what we ask for . . . well, let's just say you won't be seeing Ms. Korenz in your lands again."

Ava panned the camera over, showing Zoe Korenz in the cell, before shutting the camera off. She took the camera back up to the workshop and then joined us by the cell again a few minutes later, bringing a tray with water and a bowl of salted rice for Korenz to eat. Freya unlocked the cell and set the tray down on the table by the bed. She also unlocked the cuffs we had put on Korenz. She locked the cell again as she stepped outside.

Korenz woke up a few minutes later, looking at us but saying nothing. She drank the water and ate the rice we had left on the table but continued to say nothing. She stared at the wall for several minutes before standing up from her bed and walking over to the sink to wash her hands. It seemed she was taking as much time as she could before acknowledging us. She finally pulled the small wooden chair to the center of the room, sat down, and stared at us.

"What was it you injected her with?" I whispered to Freya.

"Sodium pentothal," she answered. "It was hard to get hold of any of the stuff here, and I really didn't want to use it since it's fairly dangerous. It's been used to get people to give up information before, however."

Ava spoke quietly. "I mixed something similar into the water and rice. The effects aren't long-lasting, and she shouldn't suffer any long-term effects or damage from it."

CHAPTER TWENTY-FOUR

Korenz spoke up suddenly, harshly: "What do you want from me?"

"We're just going to ask you a few questions," I said. "We won't harm you, but you'll be kept in here for some time."

"F-fine . . . ask your questions, damn you."

"First, what are Krisprelli's further plans for Hampkurth?"

Zoe was silent for a moment and then spoke. "He's going to send two more large groups of soldiers toward Porton and Blackacre at 21:37. For whatever reason, he's decided that will be the last assault he sends to the state, even if you manage to defeat it."

"It's working," Ava whispered to me. "Keep going."

"Okay, Korenz, next question. What are Krisprelli's general plans?"

Once again, she was quiet for some time before she answered. "He's monitoring your troop movements, watching where you go, and then deciding how to act based on that. His advisors, the rest of us who can get close to him, have been telling him he should launch an attack when you're distracted fighting elsewhere, but he refused to do so. He'd rather face you all head on and try to push through rather than seize an opportunity to easily gain back ground."

"Krisprelli's never been a thoughtful man. Have you been using the underground tunnels to move troops?"

"Again, Krisprelli isn't one for surprise attacks. And he thought they were too dangerous for us to use."

"All right, last question. Where are the Royal Army members stationed when not in battle?"

"In a barracks, near Krisprelli's hold. No place you could get to without almost making it to Krisprelli himself."

"Thank you, Zoe. These answers will prove to be rather useful for us."

We left the basement where the cells were located and walked back to the workshop. Ava called an Opposition member into the room to ask him to carry the box with the corpse to the incinerator. I helped him carry it, and after we threw it into the fire, I walked back to the workshop where Ava was already back working on one of her projects.

I sat down by Freya. "A bit violent to just burn a body like that, don't you think?"

"He was Royal Army. Not like we were going to bury him," Ava replied.

"Let's not worry about that now," Freya said. "According to Korenz, we have 12 hours until more of the Royal Army marches toward Blackacre and Porton. We need to make sure the troops are prepared for the fight."

Ava put down the robot arm she was looking at. "And if we win, we'll have Hampkurth. Having Porton in our control means I'll have access to a good supply of resources and likely better machinery for my work, too."

"Yes," Freya replied, "that, too. Let's go up to the surveillance room; I'll talk to the troops there."

We walked to the surveillance room where the screens still displayed the drones' cameras as they hovered over Blackacre and Porton. Our troops were making their rounds as we sat down. Freya spoke into the comms station, informing the troops of the time Krisprelli's troops would be marching toward them. We saw the troops rush toward their supplies, making sure everything was ready and in order. They reloaded their guns and then continued their patrols since it would be several hours more until the fight.

"Ava," Freya said, "have you broadcast our video to the Royal Army yet?"

"I've not had the time to do so. I'd be able to from here, however."

Ava plugged the memory card containing the video into a computer and then connected the computer to the communications network. She masked our transmission number and modified the communications channel to the broadcast frequency of the Royal Army. With a few more key presses, Ava sent the video across the frequency. The entire Royal Army would be seeing it.

"There," Ava said as she sat back down, "it's been broadcast. Every one of Krisprelli's soldiers wearing their armor should be seeing it. Once it's finished playing, I'll set the comms frequency back to our own."

Ava disconnected the computer from the comms system, took the memory card out of the computer, and destroyed it. After a few minutes went by, she fiddled with the comms system, unmasking our transmission number and setting the frequency to our own so we could communicate with our people. We stayed in the surveillance room for several hours. Ava brought us meals every now and then. It was nearly time for the attack to occur when suddenly, every screen in the surveillance room went black before a Royal Army soldier appeared.

"Krisprelli says no deal. Do what you wish to Korenz; we care little about her."

The screens went back to the drones, showing our people in position for the fight. A few more minutes passed, and we saw a sea of white armor marching toward our people. There were easily hundreds of Royal Army forces marching toward both cities, and our people began firing on them, taking them out. Grenades helped take out larger groups, though some were hindered by one of the RA soldiers jumping on them, shielding everyone in the vicinity. The Royal Army threw grenades of their own at our people, though only one was able to harm anyone. Our soldiers were able to run away from the rest of them.

Some RA snipers took position partway into the battle, allowing them to take out some of our people before our snipers took care of them. Both sides threw more grenades, which injured both the Royal Army and Opposition forces. The fighting continued for several hours, well past midnight, but the Royal Army forces were still numerous. Our people continued fighting until the sun began to rise, and only then did the number of Krisprelli's forces begin to decrease.

Ava and Freya had both fallen asleep in their chairs. I had barely managed to keep myself awake by ingesting caffeine pills. It was 9:12 in the morning by the time the fighting was done—nearly 12 hours had passed. The streets of Blackacre and Porton were lined with corpses, both Opposition and Royal Army. Our people had treated the injured during the battle whenever there was a moment of downtime. Most injuries were treated in time so they did not become deadly, but some soldiers succumbed to their wounds, according to what the surviving troops said through the radio. It had been a heavy price, but Hampkurth belonged to the Opposition now. I sent several trucks to Porton and Blackacre to bring our people, along with the dead and injured, back to base, keeping myself awake long enough to welcome them back, help carry the injured to the medical ward, and take the dead to the morgue. I then slowly made my way back to my room, falling asleep almost as soon as I hit the bed.

CHAPTER TWENTY-FIVE

Somehow, my exhaustion was strong enough to keep me asleep for nearly an entire day, and I woke up the next morning. It seemed quiet in the base for the first time in quite a while. Nothing had been left in my room, and no one had disturbed me. I stayed in bed for a few minutes longer and then got up. After getting dressed, I sat at my desk and wrote down a few small thoughts in one of my notebooks before leaving my room. Starving, I headed to the dining hall and made myself a meal that consisted of more than a drink and some bread.

The dining hall was rather empty this early, and only a few others sat at a table across the room from me. I took some time eating my meal, enjoying the calm feeling of the morning. Feelings like that weren't common around here, though whenever they did happen, they weren't long-lasting. Ava and Freya walked into the dining hall a few minutes after I began eating and sat down at the table with me. I kept eating as they spoke.

Ava grabbed some juice. "You slept for, frankly, an abnormal amount of time, Nate. You all right?"

"What? You didn't sleep for an entire day? You just have to try a bit harder." I smiled.

"Be serious, Nate," Freya said, sounding annoyed. "There's something Ava brought to my attention that I don't think any of us really considered as it was happening."

"Yes," Ava interjected. "When that transmission came through in the surveillance room, the one from one of Krisprelli's soldiers, how were they able to broadcast that here? I masked our broadcast channel. They shouldn't have been able to broadcast anything back to us."

"Obviously," I answered, "they decoded it. You said it yourself. Krisprelli has talented coders working for him. They intercepted our broadcast and used it to crack the masking and send the reply to us."

"That would make sense. It's likely the actual answer, too. This is incredibly dangerous for us, though. If they have the channel needed to broadcast to us, they could send harmful code to our computer systems."

"Korenz said it herself," Freya replied. "Krisprelli doesn't like surprise attacks or hits done in secret. He prefers direct combat. He wouldn't attempt to harm us with something like that."

"I suppose you're right," Ava said, "but we can't be entirely sure Korenz was accurate in stating that. I'll work in the surveillance room to modify the broadcast channel to try to protect us. Once that's done, we'll see what else we need to do today."

Freya and Ava sat at the table, allowing me to finish my meal. Once I was done, we left the dining hall and went up to the surveillance room. Ava knelt beside the communication station and got to work. Freya and I sat down in a couple of the chairs. After some effort, along with moving several parts around inside the machine, Ava stood up from the station and sat with us.

"There! Our broadcast channel is changed now. Krisprelli shouldn't be able to send anything to us again."

"And what about our soldiers, Ava? How will they communicate with us?" Freya asked.

"I sent a signal out across the base. It flipped the comms signal in the soldiers' armor to the new channel. Their comms will be uninterrupted."

"Good. We'll need those comms soon."

"What for?" I asked.

"We'll need to go back to fighting soon. We can only realistically afford a few more days of rest."

"And do you already have plans ready, Freya?"

"Not yet, Nate. We'll be going into Cheson, but I have no specific plans drafted yet. I'll start work on them later today, maybe tomorrow."

"I was hoping we could go to Porton," Ava said, "to look for supplies and resources, maybe new machinery for me to use."

"Yes," Freya replied, "we should do that. Outfitting the workshop with the best of what we can find is necessary."

"We could likely find some blueprints, too. Weapon designs, maybe armor schematics. Not sure how helpful any of it would be for us, but it would be good to look for them. Other than blueprints, there'd definitely be a good supply of resources for me to use in my work. What I'm mostly looking for, however, is one of their computers for me to slot an AI chip into and then get the code for it."

"And what do you need that for?" Freya asked.

"I can use it to produce a more stable neural link between the mechanical exoskeletal limbs, such as your legs, and the user."

"Hmm. Sounds promising. How long do you think it will take you to have the work done?"

"A day or two for prototyping, then another day to sort out any issues."

"Don't push yourself too far, Ava."

"I'll be fine, Freya." Ava squeezed Freya's hand and quickly released it.

"We should check on Korenz," I said. "We haven't spoken with her since yesterday."

"Two days ago, Nate."

"Ah, right. In any case, we should check on her."

We went down to the basement and looked in Zoe's cell. At first, it seemed she was simply asleep, so we began to leave the basement. As

Freya and I walked up the steps, however, Ava noticed that something about Korenz seemed . . . off. Freya unlocked the cell, and Ava went inside. She checked Korenz's pulse and found that she was dead.

"How did she die?" Freya asked, stepping into the cell.

Ava investigated the body. "There aren't any outward wounds. Possibly a disease, but more likely a poisoning."

"Self-inflicted?"

"Quite likely, yes. She probably committed suicide so as not to continue giving us information. I'll perform a toxicology report to find poisons."

Ava and Freya carried the body up the stairs and into the medical ward. Freya and I sat in a separate room and watched as Ava took some blood, put it in a vial, and put that into a centrifuge. A few minutes later, she took the vial and poured the contents into another machine. After another few minutes, Ava turned to Freya and me.

"She ingested bloodroot and cyanide. The cyanide is what caused her death. The amount of bloodroot she ingested was only enough to cause nausea and unconsciousness. I'm not sure why she would have ingested it along with the cyanide."

"What are we going to do with her corpse?" I asked.

"Bury it in an unmarked grave far from the cemetery," Freya answered.

"Or just burn it," Ava said.

I left the room for a few minutes to get a coffin. It took me a few minutes to find one, but once I did, I carried it back to the medical ward, and Freya helped me put Zoe's body in it. Ava then helped us carry the coffin to a truck, which drove us an hour away from the base. We dug a grave, put the coffin in it, and covered it up with the soil.

After we got back in the truck, rather than having the driver bring us back to Esterden, we requested to go to Porton. We weren't sure exactly what we would be looking for, and we were mostly going to help Ava while she searched for what she needed. The drive to

Porton was long from where we buried Korenz, and we had little to do to pass the time as we rode. We talked for a while.

"What are we looking for, Ava?" Freya asked.

"Weapon and armor blueprints, machinery, mechanical bits and bobs, resources I could use for constructing various projects, those sorts of things. Most important, however, is a coding computer. It'll have a slot for me to load one of the AI chips into so I can see its code. It'll give me a chance to work on my coding skills while simultaneously allowing me to improve the neural link tech for mechanical limbs."

"You seem rather committed to making these mechanical limbs as good as you possibly can make them, Ava," I said.

"Of course, Nate. Making weapons and armor? That's not what I want to do. It's just what I've had to do. I want to help people. These mechanical limbs were my main project before the war began, and they're the best way I can possibly help since I already have a basis for the work needed to make them. Of course, I also made the Sanitatem and the other meds. I've done a lot to help people already, and I want to continue to do so after the war, too."

"You're an incredible woman, Ava," Freya said. "I'm sure you'll continue to do a lot of good once we're out of this mess."

The rest of the ride went along fairly quietly with a bit of small talk here and there. We arrived in Porton some time later, and the driver of our truck said she would wait for us while we did what we needed to do. We first went into what looked like a factory, a fairly recent one at that. The outside of the building was damaged in places from the fighting that had occurred, but the inside appeared undisturbed.

Ava began walking around. "A place like this should have almost everything we're looking for. Let's get to searching."

We looked around the factory for an hour, searching thoroughly for what Ava wanted. Freya helped Ava pull machines out from their places and load them into the truck while I found several boxes of assorted mechanical bits I was sure Ava could use. I carried them to the truck, making sure they were safe where I put them. Ava and Freya came back inside, and we continued looking, finding more mechanical bits that Ava looked through and then picked out some specific ones.

"No coding computer in here," Ava said as she stood up. "No schematics, either. I expected as much, though. Let's go to one of their research labs. There's one just across the city."

We walked through the streets of Porton for several minutes until we came across a sleek-looking building, which Ava recognized as a research laboratory. We went inside, finding that the lab had been thrown into disarray. After digging through the mess for some time, we found hard drives and storage devices, which Ava put in a crate she found. We also came across other physical papers and documents that had designs and schematics for weapon and armor ideas, which Ava said she would look at in detail back at the base.

After searching for half an hour, we found the main object of our search: the coding computer. Ava and Freya carried it to the truck together while I carried the crate with the storage devices and documents. We rode back to Esterden, which was not nearly as long of a drive as we had taken to Porton. Once we were back at the base, we worked to carry the computer, other machines, mechanical pieces, and the crate with the storage devices and files into Ava's workshop.

Ava had Freya and me help her move the machines where she wanted, and she got them set up once they were in place. She took the crate with the files and hard drives and put them on her table. Ava also spent some time going through the hard drives and other storage devices but found nothing of great use. After looking over the schematics we found, she set aside only two that she deemed worth the time to consider. One was for an interlocking plate system for armor, allowing more mobility, along with thicker plating over more vital areas. Another was for an advanced propulsion system for guns, allowing projectiles to fly faster.

"I can combine the armor schematic with the thick alloy plating I created for our armor," Ava said, "and the propulsion system for the weapons should be easy enough to build."

CHAPTER TWENTY-FIVE

"Will you have the parts you need to construct them?" I asked.

"Definitely. The factory in Porton had plenty of resources. I could likely build gravity wells into every suit of our armor as well as the interlocking plating, build the propulsion system for all our weapons, and still have some materials left over."

Freya took a seat. "And the AI chip?"

Ava said nothing as she set up the coding computer and slotted the chip into it. The screen flashed on with a progress bar slowly counting up. It wasn't moving incredibly slowly, though it wasn't moving very quickly, either. Ava asked Freya and me to go to the barracks to bring her a few of the suits of armor and some weapons. As we brought them into the workshop, Ava was assembling some materials and tools.

As the progress bar on the coding computer ticked along, Ava constructed a small machine, which she then attached to one of the pistols. She aimed it at one of the suits of armor, and we watched as the bullet she fired went through it entirely. Ava took the ammo out of the gun and laid it down on the table. She spent a few minutes repairing the armor, taking it apart and machining it in several places. She spent some time installing gravity wells in it and putting together the interlocking plates according to the schematic.

Taking apart another suit of armor, she noted, "It's a good thing for us that the Royal Army wasn't able to get those propulsion systems for their own weapons. We'd have suffered several more casualties if they had."

"Yes, quite fortunate for us they weren't able to put it into use," I said.

We stayed in the workshop for some time while Ava worked on a few more suits of armor and built more of the propulsion systems for the weapons. Once she finished with everything we brought her the first time, we carried more of the suits and weapons to the workshop. Eventually, the progress bar on the computer finished, and the screen displayed the code.

"Here we go," Ava said excitedly. "This is what I needed. With some time, I'll have what I need to construct a better neural link device."

We watched as Ava dug through the code to find the right information, combining it with her own coding and programming on a separate computer until she had a finished project. Next, she went over to the machinery we had brought in and fabricated a small device that looked similar to the one Freya had on her to use the mechanical legs, although it looked a bit sleeker in design. Ava connected it to the computer she was performing her coding on and uploaded the code to it. She took the device and then walked over to Freya.

"This is just a prototype," Ava said. "I'll sort out issues with it tomorrow, once I've finished the armor and weapons. For now, let's just see how it works."

Ava took the device off Freya's neck and attached the new one. Freya stood up and walked around for a bit, her movements somewhat jerky, but she was able to walk around the room and return to her seat. Ava took the device from Freya's neck and put the old one back on. She made a few small adjustments to the code but returned to working on the armor and weapons. Freya and I went with her to the barracks and helped her bring back every suit of armor and weapon we had. She got to work on them while telling Freya and me we should go to our rooms and get some rest. We told Ava good night and left the workshop.

Freya walked to her room, and I went to mine. It was not incredibly late at night, though getting some rest would be good. Ava would likely work harder than she had to in order to have the armor and weapons ready tomorrow. She was also working on the neural link. Ava's work was important, but I did think she worked too hard sometimes. I wouldn't try to stop her, though, as it would be a waste of time to attempt to do so. I figured tomorrow would likely be a day of planning before we went back into Krisprelli's territory. As I fell asleep, I thought of how close we were getting to Krisprelli.

CHAPTER TWENTY-SIX

I woke up the next morning after sleeping in just slightly. It was quiet again that morning, though I knew today would be a busy one. I went to the dining hall, made myself a small meal, and ate quickly, heading to the workshop after I was done. Ava was asleep in her chair, several modified suits of armor and weapons sitting in the workshop. Two screens were on in front of her, displaying the activities of two separate computers. I sat on one of the chairs, not disturbing Ava as she slept. Freya came inside a few minutes later and sat beside me.

"I don't know how she can work so quickly," Freya said, looking at the armor. "It looks like she's already finished work on every suit of armor."

"And the guns," I added.

"Yes, and the guns. It's almost unrealistic how quickly she can work on these things."

"She pushes herself too hard. I worry about her sometimes."

"Hopefully, after the war ends, she'll allow herself to rest properly."

"Or even just get a few other engineers to help her with her work."

"Engineers and scientists. Her work is rather multifaceted, after all."

"Yes, you're right, Freya. Perhaps even we could help her."

"Perhaps."

Freya and I stayed fairly quiet as we remained in the workshop. We exchanged some more small talk here and there but mostly allowed the only sound in the room to be the quiet ticking of a clock and the hum of the machinery. The clock read 9:27 when Ava began to rise from her seat. She barely acknowledged us. She straightened up in her chair and then left the room.

Ava came back a few minutes later after cleaning herself up and was carrying a small tray of food. She sat down near Freya and me and ate her breakfast. We let her eat and said nothing, continuing to look around the room. It wasn't long before she finished her meal and went back over to her worktable where she had been working with the computers. She began typing away, modifying the code for the neural linkage device.

Freya walked over to the armored suits. "How long did you spend working on these, Ava?"

"A few hours. Once I finished a few of them, I got into the flow of making the necessary modifications. Every suit of armor we have has been outfitted with gravity wells and the interlocking plate system we found in Porton."

"Good to hear. And the guns?"

"Same thing. All our weapons have the propulsion system attached to them. We'll be well equipped for battle once we're ready to go out again, Freya."

"Yes, we need to discuss our plans for that. My early evaluations have shown me that our most logical course of action would be to go to Cheson. Krisprelli has made it into a stronghold of his empire, and Cheson is about the only thing between us and his hold. Once we take Cheson, we'll keep our people in the state to occupy it. We'll plan here at the base, bring supplies to our people in the state, and then begin the final march to Krisprelli."

I thought carefully about Freya's words. "You're serious? We're that close to Krisprelli?"

"Don't underestimate the difficulty we'll face. Krisprelli's bolstered a large number of his forces across Cheson. There aren't any specific cities we need to hold or any special points. Nothing like that. The city of Fallburn will likely be the most heavily fortified city in the state, and if we take it, we'll have a good hold in the state, but we'll need to go throughout the state and drive his forces out."

"And after Cheson? What will we do then?"

"The three of us will join the soldiers in Cheson, bringing any soldiers still at the base who could fight with us, and we'll get ready for the final march to Krisprelli. We'll face heavy resistance as we get close to his hold, but I'm sure we'll be able to persist through it and get to the man we've sought to kill for so long."

"That'll be the day," Ava chuckled, still working at the computer.

"We'll discuss the plans in more detail later. I'll draft proper battle plans, decide where exactly our troops will go to get into Cheson. A few areas around the border are bound to be less defended than others. If I can find a few, it will allow me to plot paths into the state."

Freya and I sat back down as Ava continued working at the computer. We talked a bit more about what we could do in Cheson and where we could go after that. I think I was only just beginning to truly recognize how close we were to ending this war, how soon I would be able to take Krisprelli's life, to take the revenge I'd thought about for so long. What would I do after the war was done? What kind of life would I have to return to?

Maybe worrying about the future wasn't worth the time right now. For now, I needed to focus on the present, which was currently Ava working on a computer while mostly ignoring Freya and me. We kept sitting by ourselves, minding our own business, while Ava worked. Another hour passed before Ava got up from the computer. She uploaded new code into the neural link and walked over to Freya.

"This should have sorted out any issues with the code from before. Let's try it."

Ava took the device from Freya's neck and attached the new one once again. Freya got up and walked around the room, her movements this time much more fluid and natural than when Ava was testing the new code yesterday. Her movements actually seemed a bit more natural than when they were using the original link chip. Freya walked back to her seat and sat down.

"They still feel like legs," Freya said, "though I suppose that's a good thing."

"You can keep using that link chip," Ava said as she walked back to her worktable. "The original is definitely worse."

"Thank you, Ava."

"What are we going to do now?" I asked.

Freya stood up. "What do you mean, Nate?"

"Well, Ava's done with the major projects she has been working on, and you said we need to begin planning."

"Yes, of course. We should take these weapons and armor suits back to the barracks, though. No use keeping them away from the soldiers."

Ava, Freya, and I worked together to carry the armor and guns back to the barracks, which took a few trips. We took some time to tell the troops about the modifications Ava had made to their gear and then went to the planning room. Ava took out a map and spread it on the table. It clearly showed the division of Opposition and Krisprelli territory. We had the upper hand in terms of territorial holdings, but to actually take Krisprelli would require overwhelming his troops.

"As you can see," Freya began, "Cheson is the one point holding the line between us and Krisprelli's territory. However, he's recognized that, too, and has made the state into a compound crawling with his people. Infiltrating the state will be the most difficult task we've undertaken yet."

"And," Ava began her reply, "what will we do once we've taken Cheson? If Krisprelli's fortified it to this degree, he won't allow us to hold it easily."

"We'll have forces hold Fallburn since it's the most fortified city. We'll have the rest of our people march around the border, firing upon any Royal Army forces that approach. Our people will have to remain in Cheson while we plan for the final march to Krisprelli's hold. Once we're ready, we'll go to Fallburn with the soldiers still at the base who aren't injured and bring supplies."

"And then we'll begin the march to Krisprelli?" I asked.

"Once everyone's ready, once we're ready to begin the end of this damned war, then we'll go."

"It's really almost over. We're this close to killing Krisprelli. It feels unreal," Ava said, nearly crying.

"We'll have our revenge soon," Freya said, "and we'll be able to finally make Krisprelli pay for his actions."

I got up from my seat. "His blood won't bring back our losses."

"Of course it won't, but maybe it will bring some peace to their souls. We'll return Walneyria to peace and carry the country on in honor of those who died for us."

"I'm not taking any position of power," Ava said. "You two can, if you wish. But I'm getting a proper workshop set up to keep doing my work."

Freya continued looking at the map. "Of course, Ava. We'll all be free to do what we want after the war."

I still wasn't exactly sure what I would do once the war was over. Political office was never something I considered much, although it wouldn't be entirely unfitting for me, considering I was essentially the president of the Opposition States. I could see Freya doing well in a position like that if she chose to run. Most of the governorships in the country would likely remain as they are now, with a few states replacing governors who supported Krisprelli. Things like that were likely best left to be considered after the war ended.

"I did some scouting with the drones," Freya said. "I counted five spots along the border that the Royal Army isn't guarding as heavily. We'll divide our troops into five large groups of equal size and send them through these points. As I said before, there aren't any specific points we need to take; we just need to get into the state and drive out the Royal Army."

"And how long do you think that might take?" I asked.

"If we can do it correctly, a few days. Our people will march through the state and kill any Royal Army they come across. They'll get to Fallburn, take it, and leave one group in the city to hold it. The other groups will continue to patrol throughout the state and keep taking out Krisprelli's forces."

"And once the Royal Army is out of Cheson?"

"We hold the state," Freya explained. "I'll plan how we'll move toward Krisprelli's hold, we'll all go to Cheson with supplies, our people will get what they need and rest one more night, and then we begin the final battle."

"And Krisprelli?"

"He'll die when the final battle ends."

"And who will be the one to take his life?"

"You, Nate, assuming he's not killed in any crossfire, that is."

"Are you sure you'll be ready to go back into battle again?"

"She'll be fine," Ava said, "she's recovered as much as she can, really."

"What about her legs?"

"I can walk without the exoskeleton legs," Freya answered. "They don't even really give much assistance anymore."

"That's right," Ava said. "She's mostly still wearing them because I asked her to. I wanted to see how the new link device worked over the next few days, see if there's anything further I need to modify on it."

"Ah," I said. "I see. Well, then, Freya, when will our people go into Cheson?"

"Tomorrow. I don't really need to plan anything this time beyond the entry points. The mission in general is just to get in, take out the Royal Army, and hold the place. Can't really get much simpler than that."

CHAPTER TWENTY-SIX

"Understood. What should we do until then?"

"I suppose we could just pass the time in a few more fun ways, nothing serious. You didn't have anything else you needed to work on right now, did you, Ava?"

"Nothing specific, no. I'd be glad to spend the rest of the day with you two."

We left the planning room and went to the dining hall, getting a decent meal and spending an hour eating and talking with one another not thinking about serious things in that moment. Soon enough, we'd return to battle and bloodshed, but for now we didn't have to think of that. We went to Ava's workshop and played a few card games for some time until it was late. After another few hours chatting, we went to our rooms to sleep.

It was a bit scary thinking about how close we were to ending this war, how close we were to killing Krisprelli. I thought my fears would calm down once we got this close to our enemy, but they seemed only to intensify. How would I feel once Krisprelli was actually dead?

CHAPTER TWENTY-SEVEN

I woke up early to the sound of someone knocking lightly on my door. I got up and tidied myself to look at least somewhat presentable. Then I went to the door and opened it to see Ava with Freya standing behind her. Ava grabbed my wrist and pulled me into the hallway, and the three of us walked to the dining hall. We each made ourselves a plate of food, nothing too large but enough to keep us full for some time, and sat down at one of the empty tables to eat. There were a few other Opposition members sitting at other tables throughout the room, but they were keeping to themselves or talking with the others at their tables.

"Two more hours," Freya said, "and then our soldiers will leave for Cheson."

"Why that time specifically?" I asked.

"It gives them plenty of time to prepare, but it's also the time when our entry points have the least amount of Royal Army forces in close proximity."

"I see. And what exactly will our people do once they're in the state?"

"They're bringing in suppressed weapons," Ava said. "They'll take out any Royal Army they come across as they progress through the state. At least that's what Freya told me."

"Yes," Freya said, "that's the plan. We don't want to attract the attention of the entire Royal Army that's in the state; hence the use of suppressed guns. They'll progress to Fallburn, taking out any enemy forces along the way. Taking Fallburn will be a difficult and lengthy battle for us."

"It's necessary," I said. "We take Fallburn, we open up our path to Krisprelli."

"Yes, and once we have that path, we take it, begin an even larger battle as we approach Krisprelli, and several people will be killed and injured in the process. It's fantastic."

"None of us are happy to do that, Freya."

"I know that, Nate. And I'm ready for this war to be over, but it's hard not to think about how many more will die when we're this close."

"We'll be okay," Ava said, uncharacteristically optimistic. "I'm sure of it. Our people will take Cheson, we'll rest and prepare to join them, we'll go to Fallburn, we'll march to Krisprelli, and we'll end this war for good."

Freya finished eating. "Well, it sounds so simple when you lay it out like that."

"I'm not trying to say it'll be easy, Freya. Not even close. I was simply saying how close we are to ending this all. How close we are to being able to return to peace."

I got up from the table. "What are we even going to do in peace? Have any of us really thought about that?"

"I've already told you," Ava said. "I'm getting a proper workshop, hiring people to help me, and continuing my work."

"I've not really thought much of it. Maybe I'll run for office," Freya said.

Freya sounded like she was joking when she said that, but I felt as if she were telling the truth. I could see her doing well in office. I hadn't thought much about what I would do after the war. Return home, maybe. Find someone to start a new family with—once any major work I would need to do was finished, of course.

"Thinking about the future isn't worth anything to us right now," Ava said as she stood up. "Let's go get the troops ready."

Freya and I stood up and walked behind Ava as we left the dining hall. We made our way to the barracks where a few soldiers were sitting around. It was still fairly early in the morning, so most of them were in their rooms sleeping. We had not told them they would be returning to fighting today, so none of them had gotten ready. Freya hit the button to assemble the troops in the main room of the barracks, and a few minutes later, they all arrived. Some of them were able to infer what we were about to say from the fact that the three of us had collected everyone together so early. Most of them, however, waited for us to speak.

"Today," Freya started saying, "you will be marching into Cheson, the final barrier between us and Krisprelli. He's essentially made the state into a compound crawling with his soldiers, with the border carefully monitored. Krisprelli has, however, left a few weak points in his security. There are several points along the border relatively undefended. In around an hour and 40 minutes, they will be at their least guarded. That's when you'll go to the state and begin taking out the Royal Army that's inside. You'll be using suppressed weaponry; we don't want to attract any more attention from Krisprelli's forces than necessary. The goal is simply to drive his forces out of the state. We have no specific points to capture anyone this time. Taking the city of Fallburn, however, is a goal. It would allow us a heavily fortified point in the state, and we could defend it easily enough."

Our troops began getting their gear ready, putting on their recently modified suits of armor and taking their guns, also recently modified. They had two sets of weapons: one suppressed and one not. The suppressed weapons were a pistol and submachine gun, while their unsuppressed guns were a rifle and revolver. The snipers simply attached suppressors to the guns they normally used.

Ava made sure the troops had the gravity fields of their suits turned on, while Freya made sure they had their gear in check. Once everyone had their armor on and guns ready, they packed the rest of their supplies—ammo, rations, and medical supplies. It took about 20 minutes for everyone to be completely ready. Riding to the points along Cheson's border would take around half an hour, giving the troops another 50 minutes at the base to prepare themselves before they had to go out.

We talked with the soldiers for some time before leaving the barracks. They didn't seem particularly excited or happy to be leaving again, which was understandable. Going out into battle, getting so close to death, is not something one particularly yearns for. We went up to the surveillance room and sat down. Freya carefully navigated the drones toward Cheson, keeping them out of the Royal Army's sight. After more time passed, our people boarded the trucks that would take them to Cheson's border.

Ava watched the drone's camera. "How many of Krisprelli's soldiers are in Cheson, Freya?"

"He has hundreds spread throughout the state," Freya answered. "Around 250 in Fallburn specifically, at least the last time I counted. It was difficult to get an accurate count, though, so there's likely a fairly large variance between that estimate and the actual number."

"And how many of our soldiers did we just send to the state?" I asked.

"There were 232 with 47 able-bodied soldiers still at the base in the event we are attacked here."

"We only have 279 soldiers left to fight for us?"

"There are another 16 soldiers recovering in the medical ward, so 295," Ava said.

"We've lost a lot of people during this war," Freya said. "We gained only a few more soldiers when we took another state into our territory. The fact that we've done as well as we have with as little as we have is quite fortunate."

"We'll just need to keep fighting, then," I said. "We won't allow our losses to slow us down. We'll just keep marching to Krisprelli's hold until he's dead."

"Well said, Nate. As long as we don't give up, we'll fight in the name of those who died for us until Krisprelli's been taken out."

"Krisprelli will burn for what he's done to us," Ava said intensely. "May his death be painful."

Another few minutes passed quietly as we'd run out of things to say. We saw a few patrols of Royal Army on the drone cameras, but they were small patrols. Freya said the patrols were larger near the cities and especially closer to Fallburn. We waited a little while longer until we saw one of the patrols get taken out. We saw one of the groups of our soldiers enter the frame on a drone's camera, and Ava took control of the drone to follow them.

Our troops continued marching throughout Cheson, carefully avoiding the eye of Krisprelli's patrols. They cautiously took out the Royal Army soldiers when they were sure it was safe to do so and continued to march forward once the patrol was dead, hiding the bodies to prevent later patrols from finding them and knowing we had gotten into the state. All five groups went about this way until the sun began to set. Three of the groups reunited in the town of Acorith, clearing out the few groups of Royal Army forces in the town. The other two groups worked together to clear out the city of Eanverwich, which was also lightly defended.

The groups in Acorith and Eanverwich both set up camps on the top floors of the tallest buildings in the towns. A few went up to the roofs to watch for the Royal Army, though they saw none as it became darker. After a few hours, another group went up to the roof, while the first group went back down to rest. Ava let the drones hover over the towns as we continued watching.

"At least they have a proper place to rest for the night," Freya said. "That's good."

"And tomorrow?" I asked.

"Tomorrow they get up, leave the towns they're resting in, and then keep marching through Cheson. Ideally, they head toward Fallburn, begin the fight, and win it with minimal losses."

"And if that doesn't happen?"

"Then they'll have cleared out more of the Royal Army, and they'll get to Fallburn the next day."

"Things will happen how they happen," Ava said, "and we'll just have to watch."

We stayed in the surveillance room for another hour or so, making some more small talk and watching our people in Cheson. Once we started growing more tired, we left the surveillance room and went to our bedrooms. I was not tired enough to fall asleep quickly, but I was tired enough that I needed to lie down. Our people had done well in Cheson today, but we still had farther to go until we could get to Krisprelli.

We were close now—very close to his hold. But that only added to the danger we faced. Cheson was heavily defended, especially Fallburn, which was where we were going. Krisprelli's hold would likely be armed to the teeth and guarded by nearly every soldier he had. The closer we got to Krisprelli, the higher the risk became. Was Krisprelli as afraid as we were? Was he in fear for his life?

Krisprelli was a twisted, evil man. I don't think he ever had a conscience since the day he was born. If he did, he had found out how to kill it. He didn't care about human life; he didn't care about the feelings of others. He only cared about himself, furthering his goals and maintaining his power. But he was becoming desperate, and it showed in his defense of Cheson. I eventually fell asleep, thinking over everything.

I woke up the next morning and went to the surveillance room, taking only a few minutes to tidy myself. Freya and Ava were already sitting down, watching the soldiers through the drones. Our people were still marching throughout Cheson, though I didn't see them running into any more Royal Army patrols. I sat down next to Freya and watched the screens.

"They're nearly to Fallburn," Freya said as I sat down. "Not much farther now."

I watched as the troops got closer to the city, its walls looking heavily fortified, rising fairly tall. The snipers carefully made it to the top of the walls using their grappling hooks and then got to the roofs of the buildings. Our ground forces sneaked inside the city and got into position. The snipers took out some soldiers while our ground forces fired. The battle for Fallburn had begun.

CHAPTER TWENTY-EIGHT

Our troops used their unsuppressed weapons since stealth and surprise weren't something we had on our side any longer. The snipers worked quickly to take out any Royal Army snipers they had missed so they wouldn't have time to shoot at any of our people, although the gravity fields around them would make the bullets essentially useless. Krisprelli's troops were quick to realize our people had gravity fields and began tossing grenades. We knew grenades could pierce the plating of the armor, but we had yet to see how they interacted with the gravity fields.

"Will the grenades harm them?" I asked.

"I'm not sure," Ava replied, "I didn't get to test that, and we've never had it happen in the field. Shrapnel would be harmless, but I'm unsure what will happen when it comes to the actual explosion."

A grenade exploded close to one of our people, the energy going through the gravity field. It damaged the plate, and I could see she was bleeding. One of the other soldiers rushed over to her, got her into a safe area, turned off the gravity field, and treated her wounds. Once he was sure the wounds weren't too bad, the soldier reenabled the gravity field. The wounded soldier remained in the safe area, while the one who had treated her went back to fighting.

"It would seem the field helps to dampen the explosion's power," Ava said, "but they still wound the soldier. That grenade also wasn't immediately next to that soldier when it detonated. An explosion in closer proximity would likely inflict more damage, potentially enough to still be deadly."

"We'll still need to watch out for explosives, then," I said.

"Yes, we will. But at least we know the gravity field slows them down," Ava said. "Our people won't need to run as far to avoid grenades now."

"Krisprelli's forces will likely realize that," Freya said. "I won't be surprised if they start to use explosions that detonate on impact. Likely more mortar shots or rocket launchers."

I thought for a moment. "We can tell our people to watch for any Royal Army using rocket launchers. Avoiding mortar shots would be more difficult, however."

"For now," Ava said, "let's focus on the fight in Fallburn."

Krisprelli's forces in the city were incredibly numerous, and it seemed as if our troops were barely making a dent in the Royal Army's numbers. Both sides were throwing more grenades, although our people managed to avoid all of them except one, which injured one person. Our grenades injured and killed several of the RA soldiers in the city. We continued watching the fight, seeing several of Krisprelli's people fall, while our soldiers were barely injured.

Several more hours passed. The fighting continued, only barely calming down for a few moments at a time. More of Krisprelli's forces fell, while a few of ours were injured by grenades they had thrown. The sun began to set, though that did little to slow the pace of the fight. After another hour of fighting, the number of Krisprelli's forces in the city finally seemed to thin out. Within another hour, the city was cleared of the Royal Army. Our soldiers found places to rest and lay down for the night.

We were sure Krisprelli wouldn't allow us to take the city that easily, but for now, we didn't care. Thankfully, we hadn't lost anyone during the fight and had only received fairly minor injuries. Freya,

Ava, and I stayed in the surveillance room for some time, watching a few groups of our soldiers take time to go up on the roofs to act as lookouts.

Freya stood up. "Krisprelli's going to be sending more of his troops to Fallburn tomorrow. I'm sure of it. Likely early in the morning. He won't allow us to hold the city so easily."

I got up from my seat. "We'll see what he does tomorrow. For now, I think a good night's rest is something we could all use."

The three of us left the surveillance room and bid each other good night as we went to our rooms. It seemed that for now, we had been able to slow the approach of Mortality, to prevent it from sinking its rotten, twisted teeth into more of our people. I was sure it would have another way to start feeding once more, but for now, we had staved it off. For now, we were starving it.

Starving Mortality was only a temporary activity, however. It had a way of splintering itself off into the Royal Army soldiers as a way to give itself a physical manifestation. I supposed, however, that in the same manner, it had splintered itself into our soldiers, too. It cared little for the allegiance of who it feasted on; it simply cared about getting that meal. Perhaps once this war was over, I could kill this personification of Mortality I had built up so heavily in my head.

Soon enough, I would feed Mortality directly, deliberately, with my own hands, its final rotten meal being Krisprelli. Perhaps by ingesting the tainted, corrupt blood of that fiend, Mortality would die with him. No one could stop death, and no one could kill Mortality, but one could end its manifestation by sending it some rotten meat. That meat would be Krisprelli, and it would end the manifestation in my head.

Mortality had conjured itself into my dreams, my nightmares. I did not see it clearly but rather as a shadowy being lurking behind every corner. It kept getting closer and closer until I woke up to knocking on my door. I got up, got dressed quickly, and then answered the door.

It was Freya, who looked like she had just gotten out of bed. Ava was right behind her and looked like she had taken time to get cleaned up. I began to head to the stairs to go to the surveillance room, but Ava grabbed my hand and pulled me along as we walked to the dining hall. I made myself a small plate of food and sat down to wait for Freya and Ava.

"For now," Freya said as she sat down, "Fallburn remains uncontested, held by the Opposition. As we know well, however, Krisprelli's not going to allow that to stand for long."

I ate my food. "What are our people doing right now?"

"Patrolling the city, watching for the approach of Royal Army troops. A few are resting."

"And how much longer do you think we have until Krisprelli sends his troops forward?"

"A few hours at best," she said. "There are probably still some groups of the Royal Army who have set up camp in the state. He'll order them forward, along with more soldiers who are at his hold."

"How big do you think that battle will be?"

"Big. Likely comparable to the battle we fought to take the city, if not bigger. I would expect impact explosives this time, assuming Krisprelli's forces were able to figure out they would be able to kill our people or at least seriously injure them."

"It would kill them," Ava said, finishing her plate. "A direct hit with an explosive would have enough force to kill, even with the gravity field."

"It's impossible to completely evade the clutches of Death," I said mournfully.

It kept finding ways to feed. Cutting off one method of its nourishment just encouraged it to find another. I would kill Mortality, even if it was the last thing I did in this life. It couldn't be a permanent death, for one can't bring death to Death, but I could at least stave it off for the time being. My personification of the fear of death—it would die with Krisprelli. Perhaps it was foolish of me to still occupy my mind with thoughts of this being I created, but it was difficult not to think of it. For now, however, I needed to focus on the physical enemy at hand: Krisprelli.

"Are you all right, Nate?" Freya asked.

"Uh . . . yeah, I'm all right. As good as I can be right now, really."

"That's good. Come on now, we need to go."

We cleaned up our table and left the dining hall. We walked to the surveillance room and sat down in front of the screens, which were still showing the drones' cameras that were hovering over Fallburn. Our troops were marching through the city, and our snipers were perched on a few rooftops. For some time, it seemed as if they were sitting unopposed with no one coming for them.

Then a mortar strike hit the city, injuring several of our people and killing a few who had been unfortunate enough to be caught in its immediate blast. Another mortar strike hit soon after with the same result. Our uninjured people rushed over to those who had been injured and worked quickly to treat their wounds. A few more minutes passed with no further mortar strikes hitting and no Royal Army approaching, at least not immediately.

We watched as our people rushed to cover, getting into position for further battle. Our snipers prepared themselves, watching for Royal Army soldiers. A few more minutes passed, and nothing major happened. Eventually, our snipers began firing, and we saw the approaching RA forces. At first, it seemed to be only a few, but that grew to dozens and then to hundreds. Our snipers worked as fast as they could, picking off a few of them. Our ground forces began to fire at them, wounding a few of them and killing others. Krisprelli's forces continued to march forward.

We continued watching as our troops kept firing on the Royal Army soldiers who were approaching. Once again, both sides were throwing grenades. Our people managed to avoid them, while the Royal Army lost several of their soldiers to the grenades our troops threw. Krisprelli's troops didn't slow down and simply kept marching forward toward Fallburn. One Royal Army soldier had a rocket launcher and got taken out by a sniper. He was able to fire off a rocket before he died, however; and it hit the roof that a few of our snipers were on.

The explosion itself only wounded the snipers, but it caused the roof of the building to collapse. The snipers fell to the ground, dying on impact. The other soldiers and snipers were quick to find any RA troop using a rocket launcher and took them out quickly. The fight continued with more Royal Army troops approaching the city and more grenades exchanged. Our people continued to take out the Royal Army that approached Fallburn.

"At least we haven't lost all that many people," Freya said, "but this battle is taking quite some time. It doesn't even look like we've made a dent in Krisprelli's forces."

"We just need to keep fighting. I'm sure our people will drive the Royal Army out of the city soon enough," I replied.

"Let's just hope you're right about that, Nate."

And so the fight went on for several more hours until it seemed like the number of Krisprelli's soldiers was actually beginning to go down. Our soldiers continued taking out the RA forces firing on them, and a few hours later, it seemed as though they were completely out of the city. Our troops continued to patrol the streets, looking for more soldiers, while our snipers and other soldiers stood guard, watching for more.

"We need to go," Freya said. "We don't know how long we'll have this hold on the city. We have to go now and get ready for the final march. And then we end this war."

We were close, incredibly close, to Krisprelli. If everything went according to plan, he'd be dead by the end of tomorrow, and the Opposition would win the war. It was a strange feeling, almost surreal. I was ready for all this to be over, ready to calm down. We left the surveillance room and went down to the barracks.

CHAPTER TWENTY-NINE

Our hold on Fallburn and Cheson as a whole wasn't firm. Our soldiers knew it, I knew it, Freya knew it, we all knew it and recognized it. We held the city and the state for now, and we had to act on our opportunity to get into the territory Krisprelli held. We didn't have a direct path, no specific directions from Fallburn to Krisprelli's hold. All we knew was the general location of our goal and which way to head.

Krisprelli's hold was a compound he had made into a fortress. It spanned nearly a mile and was reminiscent of the manor of a medieval lord, combined with a police state and military base. Krisprelli himself stayed in a smaller house, away from the major areas of his hold. It was not the size of his hold he cared for but rather making sure it was fortified and heavily defended. Getting through the walls of the compound would be difficult, but making it through to Krisprelli, taking him out, and getting out alive would be close to impossible.

As we walked, I asked, "Do you think they'll use explosives?"

"Inside the hold?" Freya replied. "I doubt it, but I wouldn't be too surprised if they did as a last-ditch effort to prevent us from killing Krisprelli."

"They'll do anything to protect him," Ava said, "as long as he's feeding them and giving them a steady supply of funds."

"Is the value of the Walneyrian dollar even steady?" I asked.

"We're still using it as currency in Opposition territory and Krisprelli's territory," Ava answered. "Although commerce and business likely didn't slow down quite as much in Krisprelli territory as it did in the Opposition States."

We continued walking as Freya spoke. "We'll worry about the economy after Krisprelli's dead. For now, let's just get our things together and get on the way to Fallburn."

As we walked into the barracks, we saw the troops who were still in the base sitting around talking among themselves. I put on the armor Ava had made for me while Ava and Freya took two of the suits from the supply. We got our guns ready, packed plenty of extra ammo, and got our other supplies together. Freya double-checked us and made sure we had everything we needed, and then we went to the front of the room.

We didn't say a word, but the soldiers knew to begin preparing their gear. They got up from where they were sitting and went to where the gear was stored. They put their armor on, got their guns ready, and then packed the rest of their supplies. As she had done with us, Freya checked their gear, ensuring nothing was out of place or forgotten. We began to leave the barracks once everyone was ready.

"What about the soldiers in the medical ward?" I asked. "Have any of them recovered enough to fight again?"

"We can go check on them. A few may have recovered enough by now," Freya said.

We went to the medical ward where some of the beds were occupied by a few of our people. Some of them still looked too injured to go into battle again, but a few others looked fairly healthy. Ava spent some time checking on them and found that three were healthy enough to go to battle. They went to the barracks and got their things ready.

Before we left, we put together a box of supplies for our troops in Fallburn—a few medical supplies, more ammo, and rations, the nicer ones we had stocked. These soldiers had opened the way for us to get to

Krisprelli and deserved to eat something good, at least for one night. After we made sure everything was in order and ready to go, I called a truck driver to pick us up. We loaded the box of supplies into the back and then got into the truck ourselves to begin the trip to Fallburn.

One of the soldiers spoke up after some time. "This'll all be over soon."

"Tomorrow," I replied, "after tomorrow, Krisprelli will be dead. We'll end this war, and we'll all go back to living in peace."

"What about the soldiers?"

"Ours?"

"Krisprelli's. What'll happen to them?"

"They'll likely remain in the military," Freya answered, "or maybe return to civilian life. Most of them were in the military before Krisprelli took power, and most are likely just fighting because they had to in order to avoid execution."

"And yet they still met their end," I said.

"We at least had the courtesy of giving them a quick death. Krisprelli would have drawn it out and made them suffer before they finally drew their last breath."

"That's what Krisprelli deserves—a slow, painful end."

"Don't be sadistic, Nate."

"Why shouldn't he?" Ava asked.

"We don't want to stoop to the same level of brutality as Krisprelli has, Ava."

"And why shouldn't we, Freya? Krisprelli's mercilessly slaughtered our friends and family, killed hundreds of innocent people, and ruined our country to twist it into his own demented vision. He is one man. If we are to be brutal to any person, he deserves it more than any other single living being on the entire planet."

"We aren't brutal killers like he is, Ava."

"Look at how many people's lives we've taken, Freya. Hundreds of people died because of us, and more will die between now and the end of tomorrow."

"I'm not proud of what we've done. I don't like how many people have died during the war, both on our side and Krisprelli's, but their deaths are necessary. Krisprelli needs to die, but there's no reason for us to be overly brutal in doing so."

"Do as you wish, Freya. I'm just ready for this all to be over."

The rest of the ride was quiet and somewhat tense. I did not think Ava and Freya were necessarily mad or upset at each other; they were both simply ready for the war to be over. Nevertheless, they didn't talk to each other for the rest of the journey to Fallburn. A few of the soldiers made small talk with one another and with me. Overall, the trip wasn't very eventful and passed quickly.

We got to Fallburn some time later and saw our troops still patrolling the city, watching for the Royal Army. The soldiers who had come with us got out of the trucks and joined the others, while a few helped us carry the box of supplies to everyone else. We talked with the soldiers, checking the injuries on those who were hurt during the fighting. They hadn't had time to be taken back to base, so we called for a truck with a few of the people from the base to bring them back, along with the bodies of the dead.

We passed the ammo and medical supplies around, making sure everyone was well supplied. We had brought enough of the luxury rations for everyone in the city to have one, and everyone was sure to give the injured theirs first. Everyone ate for a while and continued talking with one another. The transport for the injured and dead arrived after a while, and we helped the injured get inside. Then we carried the corpses. We made sure the transport got on its way safely and then sat back down.

One of the soldiers got up and began talking. "For the last several weeks, we've come together to fight against an enemy we're incredibly unevenly matched against. But against all those odds, we've ended up here, today, in Fallburn. We're here, about to begin what will be the final assault of this war. But what's important above all is that we are all here today. We have grown close to one another, and we've become friends. Most of us have lost those close to us—friends, family, loved ones. But we've made new friends in one another. Let's keep fighting to make sure that doesn't change."

I didn't know the soldier, not by name at least. That didn't detract from the value of her words, however. We had to keep fighting to protect the people we had come to care about and to honor everyone else we had already lost. The rest of the soldiers cheered at the speech, and then we all continued our conversations while eating the small meals we had brought. We finished with the food fairly quickly but continued talking afterward, helping distract us from what would be happening tomorrow.

After a few hours of conversing and enjoying each other's company, we all began making sure we had everything in order and ready for tomorrow. We made sure our guns were completely loaded and packed spare magazines so we could quickly reload our weapons. Everyone was also sure to pack plenty of medical supplies, as well as some of the standard rations we had brought with us. Once finished, we decided on places to rest but continued to talk with one another for a while longer.

"I'm just ready to return to my job," one of the soldiers said. "Hopefully, it won't have slowed down too much from the war."

"What kind of job did you have?" I asked.

"Worked in one of the factories in Hampkurth. I'm sure it'll be closed for some time to be repaired, but I'll be happy to return to it eventually."

"The factories weren't damaged too badly," Ava said, "though we did take some machines and resources from one of them. The labs in Hampkurth were a bit more disorganized, however."

"The labs always were quite a mess," the soldier said, somewhat happily. "I hope the researchers won't be out of work for too long."

"We did steal some of their research notes," Ava said.

"I don't think they'll mind too much, considering the application," I said. "They would likely appreciate it if you returned the notes, however."

"They'd probably prefer that Ava show them how she actually constructed the schematics," Freya said. "That would be a bit more helpful."

"Just don't divert too much work away from the factories," the soldier chuckled.

We kept talking a bit longer, and some of our people went to the spots they had chosen for rest. A little while later, almost everyone had gone to rest, so Freya, Ava, and I decided to do the same. There weren't really any proper beds in the city, and only a few of the soldiers had thought to bring bedrolls with them. I had not thought to do so and neither had Freya nor Ava. We'd grown used to a certain level of discomfort by this point, though, and were able to get to sleep easily enough even in less than ideal conditions.

We woke up the next morning, stretched out, and made ourselves as comfortable as we could before getting into our armor and grabbing our packs of supplies. Some soldiers came to get us, and we went outside. Everyone was ready, wearing their armor with their supply packs slung over their shoulders. We all did a quick check, making sure everyone was ready with nothing out of place. Once we were sure everything was ready, Freya began to speak, sending her voice through the comms system in the armor so she would be sure everyone heard her.

"Today, we take the life of the tyrant who ruined this country and took from us everything and everyone we cared about. Today, we end the war we've fought so hard, and we will bring the country we call home back to our ideals. Today, we bring back the ideals that make Walneyria what it is."

It was a bit hard to believe and really comprehend what we were about to do. Soon, we would march directly into land firmly held by Krisprelli. Not only that, but we would be marching directly to his hold. We would be striking directly at Krisprelli with this move, and we couldn't lose. I steadied myself, and we began to march toward our target. The war was ending today.

CHAPTER THIRTY

The direct border between Cheson and Onyxglen, the state where Krisprelli had built up his hold, was not too heavily guarded. Krisprelli had moved Walneyria's capital to Onyxglen, though he chose no specific city. He allowed the state's governor, Chester Charles, to remain in power and did not outright limit his power or influence in the state or in the country's politics as a whole. Charles fled into Opposition territory soon after the war began to avoid being so close to Krisprelli. Soon enough, Charles could return to the state he had called home for so long.

We continued on the path Freya had chosen for us. It was a long path and somewhat complicated, but she had selected it to try to minimize our chances of running into members of the Royal Army before we reached the hold. Onyxglen wasn't an incredibly developed area of Walneyria, and as such, it still had large forested areas, allowing us a decently hidden passage for our movements. We moved quietly through the trees, carefully watching for any Royal Army soldiers.

"How much farther is it to the hold?" I asked.

"Another 20 minutes or so at our current pace."

We continued along the path, still running into no one. The journey toward Krisprelli's hold seemed long, each minute feeling as if it were dragging on even longer the closer we got to our target. For so long now, we'd been after Krisprelli, waiting for the moment we could strike, waiting for the day we could take him out. Now that the day had come, it was difficult to really take it in.

As a kid, I never would have expected to be in a situation like this. I don't think anyone would think something like this would ever happen to them, let alone in a way they would become so directly and personally embroiled in it. This had all started because Ava and I had lost our family members. I wouldn't say it got out of hand necessarily, but it had definitely progressed to a point I never anticipated.

I'd seen so many people die during this war, most of them Krisprelli's soldiers, but I felt some sort of sadness even for them. Most of them likely hated what they were doing as much as we did, but they had to do it. They'd killed my family, though, and it seemed as if they could kill easily with little remorse for what they did. Now, the thought of killing Krisprelli filled me with both relief and a sense of emptiness. I would do it because it had to be done.

I'd thought about this moment many times, but I'd never really thought about how I would feel when it was this close. In a way, it felt strangely somber, not because the thought of Krisprelli's death brought me even the slightest hint of sadness, but because this was the moment we'd been building up to for so long. I wasn't sure what I would do once it was done.

Ava walked by my side. "What're you thinking about, Nate?"

"Nothing. Everything. There's just a lot to think about right now, Ava."

"I see. Just think, though. Soon, Krisprelli will be dead, we'll end this war, and . . . "

"And we'll begin a lengthy process of rebuilding the country and recovering from the civil war, repairing the political institutions of the country, seating people in positions of power, and doing everything else that will need to be done."

"None of us said it would be easy, Nate. But we can all be happy that we'll be able to end this forsaken war."

"I can't argue that point with you, Ava. I just don't know what I'll do after this is all over."

"I think you'll do well in one of those positions of power. You've done well leading the Opposition through this."

"The Opposition's been led by all of us, not just me," I said. "Besides, I don't think I'd be ready to go into a position of power like that right after the war. Maybe in a few years, after I've been able to rest and just be a citizen of a nation at peace for a while. Then I'll seek office. For now, though, I'm just ready to end all of this."

The idea of just staying in a house of my own for a while and living peacefully was a rather pleasant thought. It would be a bit longer before that would be possible, though. I'd worry about that when it was a bit closer to reality. We continued making our way through the forest, eventually coming into a clearer area, and that's when I saw it—Krisprelli's hold, its walls stretching high into the sky.

We remained in the forest, keeping ourselves out of sight while we investigated the area. There were snipers walking along the tops of the walls, as well as some soldiers who appeared to have explosives. They were waiting for us, ready to fight and prevent us from entering the hold. We slowly left the cover of the forest, keeping ourselves as hidden as possible.

What we didn't expect was a Royal Army soldier, grenade in hand, rushing out of the trees and grabbing one of our people. We were quick to react, and one of our other soldiers used a silenced pistol to take out the Royal Army soldier. It seemed, however, that was exactly what he had intended to happen. He dropped to the ground, the grenade falling with him. The soldier he had grabbed jumped on it, shielding us from the blast but dying in the process.

The explosion alerted the forces at the hold to our presence, so we sprinted out of the cover of the forest. We worked quickly to take out the ones with explosives since they were able to actually cause us harm. Our snipers used their grapples to climb to the top of the walls, firing their rifles as backup weapons to take out more of Krisprelli's troops on the wall.

The Opposition soldiers began to fire down into the inside of the hold, and then a few of them descended the wall to get inside. We heard more gunfire the next few minutes until the doors leading into the compound opened. Hurrying inside, we took cover as Krisprelli's soldiers continued to fire at us. A few threw grenades, which were easily avoided. I continued shooting until I heard another explosion. I stared at where it hit, but it took me a few minutes to realize exactly what had happened.

It hit near where Ava and Freya had been. I tried to run over, but the path was difficult as more gunfire flew my way and more explosives blew up. A few of our soldiers were able to get to the area and begin inspecting the injuries and the dead. I didn't know what had happened to Ava and Freya, and I wasn't sure I really wanted to know right now. I just kept shooting, killing more of the soldiers protecting Krisprelli.

I didn't care about the lives I was taking, not anymore, not in the way I had cared about them before. I wasn't happy to take their lives, but I didn't hesitate even slightly now. They had hurt my friends, the few people I had left in this world who were close to me. Krisprelli had already murdered my friends and my family. He hadn't done it himself, but he was instrumental in their deaths.

My parents, my brother, my other friends, Samuel—every single one of them was dead because of Krisprelli, and he didn't care about that even slightly. That damned Marcus Krisprelli, the man who was able to completely ruin Walneyria in a matter of just a few months. Maybe it shouldn't have been surprising, considering the lineage he descended from.

I kept fighting, stopping only to reload my gun. As I continued to take the lives of Krisprelli's soldiers, I progressed forward, getting closer to the house Krisprelli kept himself locked inside. I didn't care how many people I had to take out before I got into that building; I only cared about getting there. The other Opposition soldiers took out more Royal Army forces, advancing with me.

We fought for several more minutes, killing more and more of Krisprelli's forces. I was close to his house now, close to the place that would become his tomb. His forces fought hard to prevent our advance, throwing more grenades that we avoided. One had a rocket launcher, but we quickly dealt with him before he could get a shot off.

Several minutes later, we were finally there. I ordered the other soldiers to move to the side but to keep guarding me. Slowly climbing the steps to the door, I thought over what was about to happen. I was finally about to confront Krisprelli—no, I was about to kill him. I was about to kill Marcus Krisprelli, the man who had taken everything from me, the man we had been hunting for so long. I was about to become his killer.

I pushed the door open deliberately. "Well,"—I heard his voice echo throughout the empty room as I entered—"glad to finally make your acquaintance, Mr. Mair. You've all been making quite a racket out there."

Krisprelli didn't take this seriously at all. He didn't care about who died for him, the people who so quickly gave up their lives to protect his. It seemed as if he enjoyed it, as if he didn't care he was about to die. I walked toward him slowly, quietly extending the gauntlet blade. He didn't move as I stopped in front of him.

"Fuck you!" I said, slashing his face. "My family is dead because of you. My friends are dead because of you. I killed one of my friends because of you."

Krisprelli grabbed the wound I had just inflicted on him. Blood spread across his face, and it looked as if I had taken his eye with the cut. He walked slowly to his desk and picked up a large cloth that he pressed to his face to stop the bleeding. How little did he care about his life? How much did he care he was about to die?

"Nate . . . "

I stabbed him before he could say anything more. I didn't care about the words he'd say from that poison-filled mouth. There was nothing he'd have to say that was worth anything to me. He dropped to the ground, still clinging to his life of little value, his mouth twisted into a crooked smile, and I thought I saw the face of true evil when he did so.

"I was always quite interested in you, Nate. You could have done great things with the right motivation . . . "

I slashed him again. "Burn in hell, you bastard! May you be tossed into a deeper pit than anyone before you has been or anyone after you shall be."

I saw the life leave Krisprelli's body. I began to step back when I noticed he was clutching something in his hand. I peeled his fingers away from it and saw what seemed to be a remote of some kind with a single button on it. Then I heard the ticking. Realizing he had triggered explosives to detonate, I sprinted out of the house. The bombs exploded before I was out of range, and I felt an immense pain in my leg.

Some of our soldiers rushed over to me, covering my wounds and carrying me to the rest of the injured. I cared little about my injuries. There was a lot we still had to do, but for now, I was content knowing that Krisprelli was finally dead and that the war for Walneyria was over.

EPILOGUE

Ava and Freya were injured in the blast during the battle, but they survived and recovered after some time. I was bedridden for a while until Ava was able to look at my leg and the injuries I sustained from the explosion. The damage was too extensive to be repaired through surgery and physical therapy, so she had to amputate it. I had a simple prosthetic for a time until Ava was able to give me a robotic replacement.

We began the rebuilding process, fixing factories and other businesses that had been damaged during the war so people could return to work. The factories were the first to be back in working order once we returned the machines and supplies we had taken. Soon after, we rebuilt banks, grocery stores, and other places of business.

Ava did exactly as she said she would and got herself a proper workshop set up. She hired a few engineers and scientists to work with her, and she was able to begin producing robotic limbs and neural links on a larger scale. She also began producing Sanitatem Celer and gave it to the hospitals for no sort of repayment. She helped people in every way she could while not caring about her own personal benefit.

After they recovered, Freya and Ava decided to marry. It was a fairly small wedding, attended by me and some of the governors, along with a few other former Opposition members. Several new relationships, romantic and otherwise, formed between people during peacetime Walneyria. I stayed by myself, finding a small house and living the peaceful life I had imagined during the war.

Putting the political systems back into place as a democracy took some time. A few of the governors stepped in with the help of the senators who had been living in Esterden at the base. They worked with one another to put some form of government in place until we had everything ready for elections. Most of the governorships remained as they were, with a few seats changing hands due to governors stepping down or being voted out since they had been supporters of Krisprelli. Freya ran for president and won.

We began to talk with some of the people who had fought in the Royal Army, finding out that most of them were fighting for the exact reason we had suspected. They were desperate to avoid being executed by Krisprelli, so they fought, even though most of them disagreed with what he was doing. I actually became friends with some of them, and many showed remorse for their actions.

It felt strange returning to a life that wasn't much different than the one I had led before the war. It was different, of course, since I no longer had my family, but I was eventually able to get used to being without them. Freya, Ava, and I met whenever we could, which was a bit difficult since they were both busy now with their own activities.

I was happy to have this life again. I was happy not to be so used to death and bloodshed any longer. My dreams were still unpleasant at times, but they slowly became more normal and easier to deal with, even when they were unpleasant. I was sure the war had taken its toll on me, physically and mentally, but for now, I was happy. For now, I would live as well as I could in the new Walneyria I had fought to create.

JW

www.ingramcontent.com/pod-product-compliance
Lightning Source LLC
Chambersburg PA
CBHW051107030726
47504CB00006B/1823

*9 7 8 1 6 3 2 9 6 8 8 3 8 *